CONTENT WARNINGS

Kinks:

- **Ravished by Ogres:** Group sex (MFMM+) size difference, oral, anal play

- **Doubled by Dwarves:** Group sex (MFM) bondage / rope play, anal play, praise kink.

- **Exposed by The Fae:** Group sex (MFMM) exhibitionism, mind reading.

- **Corrupted by Dragons:** Group sex (MFM) monster peens, and sexy Welsh men (What? It's totally a kink!)

CONTENTS

RAVISHED BY
OGRES

ZARA JORDAN

PROTECTING
CALLBOROUGH

allborough Stronghold was a lonely place for an Incanti to live. The dark, drafty fort teetered on top of the highest mountain range in Thavalon, surrounded by fifteen-foot high stone walls and filled to the brim with muscle-bound soldiers.

It definitely could have been worse. But even with so many willing lovers to choose from, there was nothing special about the soldiers here. They were just as susceptible to my powers as any other normal man.

As an Incant, the moment any person touches me, they're enchanted to do my bidding. I don't even have control over the effect. I couldn't stop it from happening if I wanted it to, it just... does.

The last five Generals—a long line of stuffy soldiers with bushy beards and puffed up egos—were certain that the Incanti were the key to unbeatable military strength. Every defense point in the kingdom had its own small group of incants stationed along with the soldiers. We slept in the barracks, trained in the grounds... but we didn't fight in the field. Instead, we snuck in behind enemy lines, found a weak point, and charmed them over to our side.

And then, when the battling was done, we'd withdraw to our chambers and wait for the next order. Some of us might take a lover—a willing soldier, or sometimes... an unaware soldier...

But I didn't play with that fire. It wasn't enough anymore. Even when they knew what was coming to them, even when they agreed to it beforehand.

Taking a lover always felt like just that—*taking* them. And sometimes a girl just wanted to be taken.

Walking the fort wall's patrol path in the dead of night, I avoided contact with every archer I passed, keeping my gloves tugged right up to my elbows, and pressing myself flat against the wall to allow them through.

"Hey, Erin," Rayner gave me a nod as he side-stepped past me. "On night shift?"

I nodded, keeping my eye on the distant treeline.

Rayner smiled, rubbing his neck nervously. "Hey, uh, if you're free later on, do you wanna—"

"I don't do that, Ray, you know that."

"Aw," Ray pushed in, a little closer than I might have liked, and trailed a finger along the collar of my robes, tugging playfully at the cord. "We've gone through this, Erin. I'd be more than willing—"

I held up a hand, straining to hear a rumble in the distance.

Rayner frowned, lowering his voice to a whisper. "What is it?"

"Shh!" I focused on the low voices, faint parts of words floating on the wind.

"But if... Oruk... then we attack..."

Oruk... that was an Ogre's name. I clenched my jaw as my mind whirred with the possibilities. We hadn't suffered an ogre attack in years at Callborough, since long before I got stationed here. I wasn't sure the men could handle it.

They were already exhausted from the last raid of bandits we'd endured earlier that week. Even Rayner, who now looked at me like I was crazy, might have been able to battle through, under better conditions. But not today. The bags under his eyes were so dark, I could see them plainly, even in the dim moonlight.

"Never mind." I smiled, placing my gloved hand over Ray's and pushing him away gently. "Just the wind. Sleep well, Rayner."

He shook his head and wandered off, back to the barracks with his tail between his legs. There's no way he could have heard the voices—I often found I sensed things normal humans couldn't. All incants were more in tune with their senses, and I was no exception.

Once the wooden door closed behind him, I ducked low near the wall and swung my legs over the edge.

Dangling from the stone walkway, I inched along to the corner turret, where I placed my feet on a pair of rotten wooden supports. Taking the route I'd used so many times before, I picked my way down to the ground and landed softly in the bushes.

The low voices came from the edge of the treeline—a small clearing sheltered by rocky outcroppings and the natural swell of the land. There was no way the guards would have been able to see anything, even from their perch on the walls.

But once I'd crept far enough over the brow of the hill, I saw the telltale flicker of mage light. A blue orb hanging in mid-air, casting a dim, ghostly light on four gigantic bodies, clustered with their heads together and talking in low grunts.

I settled into the undergrowth and pulled my hood closer around my platinum hair, hoping it would be enough to stay unnoticed.

"I told you once, I told you a million times," the large hulking figure in front of me grunted. "I ain't seen no smaller take than that before."

"Azrog's right," another said. "We barely had a mouthful each."

"I'm still 'ungry," Azrog groaned.

"Calm your hump." A third ogre slapped Azrog on his beefy shoulder. "We'll get plenty in the morning. Just a few hours till sunup."

My breath came in fast, shallow pants as I considered what they were plotting. They were most likely aiming for the fortress, hoping to pick off the soldiers for a decent meal. Or, if they had more sense, they could have gone to the next village down, only a short way down the mountain.

I couldn't let either happen. There had to be some way of stopping them.

They were all shirtless, even on this frosty night they wore only leather pants and shoes. If I could get close to one on its own, I could charm it. Charming them all wouldn't be impossible, but it was sometimes difficult to pay attention to more than one connection at a time. Better to focus my efforts on one, maybe get it to turn the group away or even enlist them.

As I considered the strengths of a military armed with ogre footsoldiers, my gaze trailed over their massive torsos. I'd seen ogres before, but only in passing, from a distance. They often camped in the mountains, but this was the closest I'd ever gotten to one, let alone four.

Their blue-gray skin shone in the moonlight, further highlighted by their hovering magelight. At least one of them must know magic, given the orb weaving around their heads. That seemed strange. I'd never heard of ogres casting spells before.

Magic users were intelligent scholars who spent years cloistered away in libraries studying their craft. Ogres were dumb beasts with a thirst for human blood. The two definitions didn't mesh.

I decided there must be more to it. Maybe they had a magician held captive somewhere, which gave me even more reason to stop them, before someone got hurt.

"Ugh!" One ogre stood and stretched, twisting his neck to loosen it. The muscles on his shoulders flexed and rippled, sending a chain reaction down his back, right to the dimples above his rear end. My mouth dried at the sight, imagining his eight foot tall frame closing in on me, covering me in its heat...

I shook away the buzzing sensation in my body, irritated at my wayward thoughts. These were monstrous creatures, intent on killing people. Aside from my shame at having lustful urges towards such a creature, I couldn't escape the fact that I had a job to do.

"I gotta take a piss," the ogre groaned, separating from the group and trudging off down a side path. He staggered around a corner, behind a rocky cliff face.

Seeing the perfect opportunity, I sneaked after him, keeping my distance from the magelight to avoid detection. One of the magical orbs followed the ogre, hovering behind his head, lighting his path. The other three were content to talk among themselves, picking god-knew-what from between their teeth.

I closed in behind the lone ogre, humming under his breath. Slipping off one silk glove, I crept behind him. My light footsteps were easily drowned out by the loud sound of his piss hitting the cliff face.

I reached for his back and touched him, my fingers tracing the hard ridges of muscle across his lower back, finding the divot of his spine. I savored the warmth of his skin and felt the familiar rush of magical connection zip along my arm, straight to my chest. In that instant, I knew the charm had worked. We were bound.

He turned right away, not shocked, but with a look of smitten awe on his face.

"Who're you?" he asked, his cock still in his hand.

My eyes drifted down to it, illuminated by the blue magical orb above us—large and snake-like, he gripped it with a fist as big as my head. I licked my lips, flushing with shame at the excited thrill that zipped through me.

"My name is Erin," I said calmly. "I'm your friend."

He nodded. "Yes, I know. I'm Oruk."

I smiled and held out my ungloved hand again. The ogre took it, dwarfing my fingers by comparison to his huge, calloused fingers. He raised my hand to his lips and bent his head forward, planting a gentle, chafing kiss on my fingertips.

"It's a pleasure to meet you, Oruk," I said, keeping my voice as calm as possible. Inwardly, my stomach was churning—not with disgust, but with excitement. Here was a monster big enough to crush me with those massive hands, and he was treating me like a kitten he wanted to take home to pet. "Tell me more about yourself."

COMFORTING ORUK

From the moment I asked him to speak, Oruk fell into a long stream of conversation, telling me everything about himself and his travel companions.

I listened intently, expecting to hear some plans for dominating the fort or eating everyone inside. But either Oruk was not accustomed to getting to the point, or my incanti charm effects weren't as strong as I'd once thought. He gave me nothing. No clues, no plots, just endless chatter about the best way to cook up a honeybee hive, how he could turn it into a drink he called 'mead' that made you feel warm and fuzzy...

We meandered further into the forest; the ogre guided me by my shoulders, turning me down the path he wanted to take.

"Oruk," I ventured tentatively. "What are you doing here in Callborough? I haven't seen your kind here for decades."

It might have been my imagination, but I was sure he blushed—his gray-blue skin turning darker, a blur of slate stone flushing at his cheeks and all down his back. "We avoid human settlements when we can."

"Why would you avoid us?" I asked, picking across an abandoned footpath. "Don't you normally eat us?"

"Eat you?" Oruk stopped mid-step, staring at me like I'd grown a second head. "Why would we eat you?"

I considered this for a moment, frowning. "Because... you're ogres. That's..." the words 'that's what you do' stuck in my throat at the sight of Oruk's expression. He wasn't angry or confused, he was outright offended. Maybe even a little disgusted.

"I'm sorry," I said quickly, worried that my charm might lose hold. "At least, I thought that's what ogres ate?"

Oruk blinked a few times, processing what I'd just told him. Then he stared into the trees, back towards his camp. There, the other three ogres would be sitting around the fire, chatting among themselves, maybe even wondering where he'd got to.

His hesitation made me keenly aware of an imaginary hourglass in my head, dropping grains of sand ever faster, counting down the seconds until I'd be found. I had to work quicker, get more information from him, and find some way to charm the others.

"We don't eat humans," Oruk said finally, shaking off his momentary stupor. "Is that what you think of us? Is that why you run from us?"

I swallowed, nodding slowly, keeping eye contact. The second he flinched, or made any movement to hurt me, I told myself I would do exactly that—run. Sprint back to the fortress and sound the alarm.

But Oruk made no move to hurt me. His heavy brow furrowed as he absorbed this new information, and he jerked his chin over his shoulder. "I wanted to show you something."

He didn't touch me this time. Where before he'd gently pressed on my shoulder to guide me along the path, now he held back a mass of long vines that hung to the ground, as if pulling back a curtain. He stayed away from me, apparently afraid to touch me.

Afraid. Of *me*.

There was still a chance that this was a ruse, some way to get me further away from the fortress so he could trap me or butcher me. But I could still sense the warm hum of my connection to him. The incanti charm held strong, like an invisible thread connecting us to each other.

I walked under his arm, passing under the curtain of vines and into an even darker section of the forest, where the canopy was so thick no moonlight could penetrate.

"Just a few steps ahead," Oruk said gently. "Mind your footing, lots of vines on the ground."

I picked my way through, holding my hands out ahead in case I fell, until I felt a large, smooth rock right in front of me. With Oruk's quiet guidance, I side-stepped around it, on to a ledge just wide enough to walk, until the dense forest broke apart, allowing moonlight to spill through once again.

We came out onto a large rock ledge which jutted out over a massive lake. A high waterfall trickled down the stone face behind us, passing by the ledge and dropping twenty feet into the lake below. Moonlight sparkled on the water, like fireflies or a cluster of mage lights from a wizard army.

"Oh, wow," I breathed, gazing at the beautiful scene below us.

Oruk sat cross-legged on the ledge next to me. Now he sat on the ground, his head was at my eye-height, so I could better see his expression. He watched me warily, some dark thought passing over his face as he did so.

"What's wrong?" I asked, laying my hand on his shoulder.

"I had no idea humans feared us so much," Oruk murmured.

Our incanti thread hummed with his grief.

"I thought, maybe..." He looked down at his large form, raising his arms as if to allow me to take a better look.

His chest was broad and defined, sculptured as if from rock. I wouldn't have been able to circle one of his biceps with my arms, let alone his torso. His leather pants hung low on his hips, allowing a clear view of his hipbones, the way his stomach curved down low to his crotch, where a smattering of short, gray hairs curled at the waistband of his pants.

My mind flashed back to the image of him holding his cock in one hand.

I'd taken a few men in my time, but none could match Oruk, even at their most excitable.

"That's not it, Oruk," I breathed. "It's not the way you look."

"But... I'm not an idiot, Erin. I know how hideous—"

"You aren't hideous!" I said, and I meant it. I reached for his face, holding his square jaw up with both hands, and staring deep into his dark gray eyes. "You're a fine specimen of an ogre. Tall, and strong, and capable."

The ruddy flush colored his cheeks once more, and I felt a rush of fondness for this beastly man, sitting as docile as a puppy at my side.

"You really think so?" He asked.

"I really do. You're wonderful."

"So are you..." Oruk said, his eyes trailing down along my smaller form.

He took in my robes, dark midnight blue with a large hood to cover my white-blonde hair. Underneath, I wore the same leather armor as the soldiers of Callborough. It hugged every curve, molded over time to every dent and swell of my body.

And then I sensed something else over our incanti bond. A lustful warmth, burning hotter the longer Oruk looked at me.

"Your body is so tiny..." Oruk reached out to my waist, circling it with both hands, his fingers easily touching. "I wonder how you'd feel..."

"Oruk..." I adopted a warning tone, as if I was training a puppy. But I couldn't ignore the heat spreading from the incanti thread, the way it spoke to me, feeding off my own excitement. With Oruk greedily taking in every detail of my body, the whisper of desire deep inside me grew louder, until my ears buzzed with the need to satisfy it. "What are you doing?"

Oruk tugged me closer, so I stood between his legs, which he wrapped around me. The heat came off him in waves, intoxicating my senses. His hands traveled from my waist down to my ass. He cupped my buttocks and squeezed, groaning.

"You smell so sweet." Oruk leaned in to me, resting his face on my shoulder and breathing in slowly, filling his lungs with my scent. "Sweeter than honey. Are you excited, little one?"

"I—" I gasped as he squeezed again, rendering me unable to finish a single sentence.

Oruk's roving hands moved more insistently, pinching my flesh between his large fingertips and tugging at the leather straps and buckles securing my armor.

"There's no need to say so," Oruk grunted. "I can smell it on you."

He reached my front, cupping my sex with his fingertips and rubbing in small circles. The pressure from even his most gentle touch was intense, sparking arousal with no effort at all. I sank into a flood of fire—our incanti bond throbbing with lust, his heat flushing against my robes.

"Not enough to wonder," Oruk said, slipping his fingers under the waistband of my leggings. He yanked them down, cold air biting at my skin.

I moaned, goosebumps prickling along my thighs as he hoisted me up effortlessly. He lifted me by my ass, holding me up to his face and inhaling my scent again, making me shiver with need.

"I won't hurt you," he said, frowning as another dark thought passed through his mind. "I'm going to taste you, Erin. I want to drink deep from your cunt."

"Yes," I groaned, weaving my fingers through his long peppered hair and pulling his face closer to me. "Do it."

He came closer, his breath heating my sex with every low pant. "Delicious," he said in a low, gravelly voice, before dipping his head between my thighs, pulling me up to his lips like a tankard of ale.

His huge, rough tongue slaked along my sex, and I pressed against him, enjoying the scratch of his thick stubble on the insides of my thighs. I bit my lip, desperately caught between the desire to moan my pleasure to the canopy, and the knowledge that Oruk's companions were still within earshot, and would likely come running to any suspicious noises.

Or what if a soldier heard? Unlikely, but if my absence had been noted, and they were looking for me... the thought of someone seeing me in Oruk's arms made me flush with shame. But it also stoked something else inside me, some darker desire... For now, though, I had to keep quiet. This wasn't for my enjoyment, I told myself. I was only doing this to keep Oruk from harming anyone. To keep our connection strong so I could turn them all away from the fortress.

But within seconds, Oruk's attentions grew more frenzied, making it impossible to stay quiet. As soon as he'd taken one taste of me, he groaned loudly, his voice rumbling and vibrating against my pelvic bone. He shifted, holding me to him with just one hand. I looked back over my shoulder and saw him release his pants, gripping himself with his free hand and stroking slowly.

The sight of his stiffening cock made me clench with desire, a small mewl of need escaping my gritted teeth.

Oruk groaned and pressed his tongue deeper, lapping at my soaked cunt and licking me so fervently that I found myself gripping his hair, pulling him against me.

"Yes," I panted, unable to hold back anymore. I rolled my hips, grinding against Oruk's chin, rubbing my clit against his teeth and squealing at the illicit contact. I was letting a monster taste me, and I couldn't lie to myself about it anymore. I wasn't doing this as a spy, as an infiltration cover.

I was doing it because I loved it.

"Yes!" My voice grew hoarse, crying out to the canopy and competing with Oruk's rumbling grunts of satisfaction. "Oruk, I want—"

"What's this, Oruk?" A gruff, familiar voice called from the trees. "Found a tasty morsel to share, 'ave we?"

THE DREAM BINDING

"**S**he's my pet!" Oruk cried, clutching me to his chest with one hand.

I clung on to him, feeling our incanti thread strong and stable, singing with a low, burning desire that we both desperately wanted to discover with the other.

His three companions had circled us on the ledge, each showing differing levels of interest in Oruk's new 'toy'. The largest, which I took to be Azrog, looked me up and down hungrily, his eyebrow cocking when he noted my thighs, slick with arousal.

"Pets are for sharin', little Oruk," the second ogre said. "Even so, you two are makin' too much noise. The other humans will come for her."

"Why did you come this way anyway, little human?" the smaller ogre skulked over to us, poking at me as Oruk tried to keep me away. "You're too small and dainty for a soldier. Did you think you'd come kill us?"

Ignoring Oruk's protective shelter, I reached out of his hold as the ogre poked me again, and closed my hand around his outstretched index finger. Self-preservation demanded that I get all these ogres on my side, even if it meant charming them all at once.

The tug of connection pulled inside me, and I watched the frown slide off his face, replaced by warm familiarity. "Gurm," he said with puppy dog eyes. "My name is Gurm."

"Erin," I replied. "Do you want to hurt me, Gurm?"

"Of course not!" He cried. "But I don't wanna get hurt, either. Where are your friends?"

"The soldiers are all in the fortress, still," I said softly. "They don't know I came here."

Azrog and the fourth ogre stomped over to us, frowning at Gurm's sudden change in demeanor. Azrog wasted no time in reaching for my leg, stroking my naked calf with a curious look in his eyes. A combination of desire and incanti bonds boiled within me, confusing my mind with both the added connection and the desire that still throbbed in my sex.

I clutched on to Oruk's shoulder, perched on his hip, with Gurm and Azrog peering up at me curiously, and the fourth ogre frowning in suspicion. I held out my hand, but he looked at it blankly.

"What ya doing?"

"Introducing myself," I said. "Humans shake hands when we say hello."

"You humans always were a weird bunch," he sniffed, turning his back. "Come on, you lot. Not long till sunrise. Bring the pet, Oruk."

· • • • • · • • • • ·

The ogres had set up camp out of sight of the fortress, just inside the treeline of the forest. Oruk carried me all the way to the four shelters made from bent tree boughs and large furs. He brought me to his, putting me down on the ground softly and motioning inside. "You can sleep here," he said, seeming unwilling to let me go.

"Thank you, Oruk." His shelter was big enough to fit four humans—the ground covered with huge furs. I made a move to go inside, but Oruk kept a hold of my shoulder.

"Did you like it?" he asked, his brow furrowed in concern.

My cheeks flamed with embarrassment, and my eyes found the floor. Not more than a few minutes ago, he'd been calling me his 'pet'. This felt all kinds of wrong, but I had no idea how to turn him down without angering him. Plus, I wasn't really sure I *wanted* to turn him down...

"Uh, I did..." I said, clutching my leggings in front of me, keenly aware of the dampness between my thighs. "But I'm not sure it was the right thing to do... I'm a human, after all."

Oruk nodded slowly. "Sorry. But you'll stay?"

I smiled, raising up on my tiptoes to stroke his cheek fondly. "Of course I'll stay."

Just as long as I need to, to get you all to move on.

"What?" Oruk frowned at me.

My eyes must have widened in shock, because I wondered for a moment if I'd spoken out loud accidentally. Oruk looked me up and down, the line between his eyebrows deepening further. "I can hear you, you know."

"You... you can?" I felt like a heavy weight was pressing down on my chest. If Oruk could hear my thoughts... was I in trouble?

He chuckled. "You're a silly one, Erin. Yes, I can hear you. But you can't even hear yourself."

Before I could ask him to explain what that meant, he left me alone in his shelter, wrapped in furs.

• • • • • • • • • •

I moaned with bliss at the intense heat enveloping me—four massive bodies curling around me, kneading my soft flesh in their large, calloused hands, stroking and kissing every inch of my naked skin.

Their low, rumbling voices vibrated through my body, further stoking my need. I looked up into Oruk's dark gray eyes as he stroked my cheek. "You'll stay?"

"Of course, I'll stay."

He leaned down and kissed me, his massive mouth so gentle and chaste on my lips.

It's as if I had triggered a trap. Carnal instinct took over. Oruk grabbed me, pulling me against him, grinding his cock against me to force my legs apart.

Azrog cupped my buttocks, licking down my lower back as he squeezed the soft flesh, tugging gently as he moved lower.

Gurm took my hand and placed it around his cock, hard and thick, but covered in velvet-soft skin that burned with desire.

A distant roar of angry voices grumbled in the distance, threatening to wake me.

I moaned as the lust inside me grew, reaching between my legs with my free hand to stroke my clit. I woke up to find my fingers coated in slick arousal, my hand between my legs as the fantasy of three gigantic ogres fucking me faded in the morning light.

"Have at them!" the voices grew louder, a rumble of rage rolling around the forest, bouncing from the trees and disturbing my blissful sleep.

"Erin!" Oruk cried, throwing furs over me and jerking me awake. "Get up! Men are here!"

"What?" The fuzz of sleep lingered, confusing me. "What men?"

"Soldiers! Diek's angry, we need to go!"

I frowned, rubbing my eyes and peering into the foggy dawn. A stream of fire trailed from the fortress across the plains, directly towards us. Realization dawned, and I stood up abruptly. They'd be here in moments.

"Oruk," I said, grabbing his elbow and pulling him back inside the shelter. "You need to hide, now."

"No!" He cried, making a move to pick me up. "Ogres don't hide."

"They're going to kill you!" I dodged out of his reach, trying and failing to push him back.

Oruk waved his hand with a flourish, and a trail of fire followed him. My mouth fell open at the sight, realizing that the mystery mage had been Oruk all along. I just kept on underestimating them...

But the soldiers were already on us. There was no time to argue or gaze in wonder. I slipped out from Oruk's grasp, ducking under his arm and running out of the forest, still half naked. He trampled through the trees behind me, his large frame slowed by the dense bushes and vines.

The other three ogres were preparing themselves for battle, hefting clubs about their shoulders as they stomped towards the field with grim purpose on their faces.

I dodged between them, cutting in front of Azrog, so I stood between him and the soldiers, my arms wide in a protective stance.

Rayner stood at the head of the company, his face pale with panic, worry etching deep lines between his eyebrows. "Erin!" he cried. "What are you doing? We thought you were dead..."

He took in the scene—my body uncovered from the waist down, the way I stood in front of Azrog, the anger on the ogres' faces, and paused, holding back the men behind him.

"Is this...?" he raised his eyebrows at the ogres, at me, then shook his head as if clearing an annoying fly. "What is this?"

I hadn't had a plan, I just knew I didn't want this to come to bloodshed. But now the soldiers had stopped marching, I took my chance, running right at Rayner, sliding off my gloves as I closed the distance.

"Erin, what—"

Rayner's eyes unfocused the moment I touched him, but I didn't stop there, running around the small company of men, stroking cheeks, running my fingers along hands, squeezing the back of necks—finding any skin contact I could and counting the connections as I went. Three, seven, twelve, seventeen incanti threads, woven and glimmering towards me, frozen with fear, with wonder, with confusion.

I felt each and every one of them, tied to me by burning ropes. I came to a stop, gasping for breath but determined to keep the charm effects active, even if it meant losing control of the ogres.

"It's alright," I said softly to the soldiers. "Go back to the fortress. Everything is okay."

They nodded as one, their faces completely blank. All except Rayner, who stepped towards me with a curious mixture of adoration and lust on his face.

"You're leaving us, Erin?" His voice was rasping, his breath leaving huge billows of steam on the chilly dawn air.

"I am." I spoke without thinking, intensely aware of Azrog's bulky form right behind me, his breaths heavy, his stance guarded. My body shook uncontrollably, adrenaline coursing through every muscle.

Ray's mouth slackened. He took a step closer, raising his hands as if to kiss me.

But Oruk came to meet him, putting a fire-wreathed arm in front of me to block his advance. "Walk away, little man," he grunted.

Ray blinked up at him, his face paling, then nodded, seeming to come to his senses.

"Go back to the fortress, Ray," I sighed. "All of you. Just forget about these ogres. Me too... Forget I ever existed."

Without another word, every soldier of Callborough fortress turned their back on me, and walked calmly back up the hill.

I stood with four ogres at my back, watching them shrink into the distance, then file inside the fortress gates. My hands still shook, my stomach churning as I came to my senses. What did I just do? Why?

And something about the effect of the incanti charm seemed strange. I hadn't noticed it at first, but charming the soldiers made me realize—the connection to the ogres felt... different. Weaker in some ways, and stronger in others.

With the men, I found it simple enough to control, even with all seventeen of them under my thrall. But with Oruk and his companions... it almost felt as if they were the ones in control.

The fourth ogre walked a few steps in front of us, trailing behind the soldiers and ensuring they had gone. Then he turned around, looking me up and down with an unreadable expression.

"You commanded them." He said blankly.

I nodded.

He jerked a chin at the three ogres behind me. "And them?"

"I..." I hung my head. What was the point of lying, really? "Yes. I controlled them, too."

"Why?"

I swallowed the lump in my throat. "I thought you were going to eat us."

He stepped closer, forcing me to back up until I pressed against Azrog's hard, muscular thighs. My heartbeat quickened, intrusive thoughts of the night's dreams probing at the back of my imagination, threatening to make me come right there on the spot.

"Diek," Oruk said in a warning tone, holding his hand out to me protectively. "Don't—"

"I'm not." Diek said bluntly, waiting until Oruk stood down before inching towards me again. He towered over me, his square jaw set in grim determination. I felt like a soldier on inspection day. "Why'd you send the men away, if you thought we were gonna eat you?" Diek continued.

"I changed my mind." I coughed, trying to clear the shakiness from my voice. "Oruk changed my mind. We've got you all wrong. I can see that now."

With a speed I could never have expected from such a large creature, Diek reached out and grabbed my wrists, forcing me back against Azrog and pulling my arms behind me.

When he touched my skin, I expected my charm to take effect. For his expression to slacken just like Ray's. But he remained grim and determined, his keen eyes piercing, as if he was looking right into my mind. "You have got it wrong, little one," he murmured, watching my face closely. "You can't charm us. Ogres don't fall to the incanti so easily. We've got charms of our own, you see."

My heart pounded in my chest. "What? But... Oruk..."

Diek grinned, his eyes glinting with humor. "Oruk's a randy beast who'll lick anything if it's turned on." He sniffed the air. "And you are an easy one, aren't you?"

I groaned, tugging against his massive hand gripping me, but I had no chance of getting free. He slid his free hand down my body, making me shiver.

"Then we might just eat you, after all."

A CARNAL BOND

"She's mine, Diek!" Oruk growled, muscles flexing as he faced off with the giant in front of me.

Diek bristled, gripping my wrist tighter and pulling me towards him.

"You already 'ad a taste," Azrog grunted, guarding me from Oruk. "Remember your place, runt."

I wanted to defend him, speak out against their rough attitudes, but something in the way Diek held my arm was taking over. I felt the same rush, the same thread connecting us. It was just like any other incanti bond... but now I focused on it, really felt it, I realized just how different it was.

This wasn't a charm I had cast. It was more like they'd cast a spell on me.

Diek made a big show of hauling me up his body, dragging my wrist until he forced me to climb up him, straddling his hips as though I was shimmying up a tree trunk. He watched Oruk the whole time, his grin widening. "Let's see who the little human chooses, shall we?"

"Her name is Erin!" Oruk grunted.

"Well, Erin," Diek smiled at me, hugging me against him so my sex rubbed against his abs. The sparse curls of dark hair there tickled my thighs, making me hot with anticipation. "Who would you like to taste you next?"

My eyes rolled at the sound of his voice. The rumble vibrated from his body, directly to my cunt. I resisted the urge to grind against him, half dangling from one arm and gripping as tightly as I could with my thighs, although he held me securely enough. "I... I don't know," I said shakily. "I'm not used to this. This feeling..."

I was the *taker*, never the taken.

I had no idea what they would do next, and no control over them. That thought alone was enough to make me combust. The thought of them all writhing around me, grabbing at every inch of me just as they had in my dreams. Was it a premonition, instead?

My gaze fell on Oruk, who watched from behind Azrog's outstretched arm, his eyes pleading with me.

"Oruk, first," I said, smiling at him. "I want to finish what we started."

"And then?" Diek asked, rubbing his thumb in circles over my ass, pulling my buttocks apart and easing between them.

I gasped as pleasure lanced through me, my back arching, pressing me against him. "Do what you will with me," I said. "I've never been controlled, before."

"Aye," Azrog chuckled. "We'll do that and then some, lass."

Diek settled me down on the floor with more tenderness than I had expected, and Azrog allowed Oruk to come to me.

We practically collided with each other—Oruk automatically lifting me to his waist so I could kiss him. Now I didn't have to stay silent, I allowed myself to let go, rocking my hips and grinding on him as he reached for the buckles on my clothes. He tore at the straps holding my body armor on to me, snapping the buckles rather than undoing them, and peeled the leather away from my skin.

Now fully naked, every nerve ending hummed with pleasure at the contact with Oruk's heated skin. I clutched his shoulder, kissing him and tasting the salt of his sweat on my lips.

With a growl, he threw me to the ground, ensuring I landed on a soft mossy patch, and dived between my legs, lapping at my sex as if he'd been starved for weeks.

Around us, the other three ogres circled, watching us hungrily and stripping their clothing, dropping leather pants and loincloths on the ground. I became mesmerized by the sight of their cocks, long and thick with huge, bulbous heads, stiffening further by the second as Oruk slurped at my pussy.

He locked his lips around my clit and sucked—hard—bringing me to the brink of orgasm before backing away with a sly grin and sitting back on his knees. "You like this?"

"So much," I panted. "I love this. More, please."

"I want to know what you feel like," Oruk said, glancing down at his cock.

I hesitated at the sight, the unusual shape of its thick, bulbous head making me wonder whether it would even work. Would it break me open the moment he penetrated me?

But another part of me yearned for it, begged for him to be inside me, to take me.

"Yes," I breathed. "Fuck me."

Oruk groaned, punching the ground on either side of my head so hard that the ground shook from its force. He eased towards me, pushing until the pressure grew, white hot and blinding. But my pleasure grew with it, my ears buzzing with my heartbeat until I was deaf to my own cries of 'yes', and 'please', and 'more'.

Further in Oruk pushed, spreading me wider and grunting with the effort of holding back. Finally, he stopped, thrusting slightly at the end of his stroke. Deep inside me, I felt him hit a spot like fireworks, and my body trembled. I tried to wrap my legs around his waist, but I could barely hook my feet over his wide hips. Instead, I found myself spreadeagled beneath his massive bulk, panting and begging him breathlessly for more.

He scooped his hands beneath my shoulders and lifted me on to him, sinking even deeper inside me with a satisfied growl.

"Move," he commanded in a low voice.

The burning link between us pulsed—not an incanti charm, but a deep, carnal, lustful bond. I gazed into his eyes and circled my hips, gasping at the feeling of his cock deep inside me.

At Oruk's nod, Diek moved behind me, licking my back and moving down. Each lick, nibble and kiss from him stoked my desire more, until his hands reached for my ass, and pulled my buttocks apart.

"Oh, yes," I moaned, dropping my head back against his chest as he pressed against me.

The heat intensified, burning me all over as he pressed inside me, slowly stretching my ass with his ball-like cock head, making me squeal from the intensity of taking him.

Azrog moved in on my right, Gurm on my left, both of their cocks hard and ready. I reached out and took one in each hand, pumping them slowly and grinding between Oruk and Diek as they growled their encouragement.

"Such a tight cunt," Oruk moaned. "I wanted to have you for myself, Erin. But you're so hungry. You want us all, don't you?"

"Yes!" I screamed, "I want you all."

"Do you reckon you could fit all of us inside you at once, little one?"

My eyes rolled at the thought, and I tightened my grip on Azrog and Gurm, smiling at their grunts of appreciation.

"I don't know," I breathed, rocking between Oruk and Diek as they found a rhythm inside me. "I doubt I could, but I'd want to."

"Of course you would," Azrog murmured, gripping my hair and turning me to face him.

I opened my mouth willingly, gazing up into his face. His lip curled with satisfaction, and he guided me on to his cock, chuckling when I almost choked on him.

Oruk and Diek became more frenzied, thrusting in turn with each other, so I lost all sense of time or place. All I knew was the sensations they gave me.

Behind me, Gurm reached for my tits, pinching them so hard I squealed with pleasure.

The four of them laughed, stroking my ass, my shoulders, my neck, my face... we became such a tangle of hands and limbs and cocks that I couldn't keep track of who was who anymore. I climbed again, soaring higher on adrenaline as they passed me back and forth, taking turns with my mouth, bouncing me between them.

Soon, Azrog gripped the back of my head, fucking my face until I could barely breathe. He groaned, his hot seed coating the back of my throat before he released me. I sucked in one lungful of air before Gurm turned my face to him and did the same, gripping me by my jaw and muttering dark words of encouragement for my ears only.

"You want more, little one? You want us all to feed you with our salty seed? I'll shoot my load right in the back of your throat until you gag on it..."

I moaned, sucking hard as he pumped into my mouth, his salty tang covering my tongue and rousing my excitement yet again.

Diek clutched at me, his fingers digging in to my flesh as he found release inside me, sending me flying once more, crying out my orgasm to the birds in the trees, not caring for witnesses. I met their thrusts with my own, grinding against them, whispering into Oruk's ear. "I want it. Give me your cum. I want to feel you dripping between my legs for the rest of the day. Take me until I'm stuffed full with you—"

Oruk clenched his jaw and pulled my hips, grabbing me roughly and thrusting inside me harder than ever, pushing so deep that I saw stars. He stilled, groaning as he pumped thick streams of cum inside me. Still, I was bonded to all of them, unable to move, *unwilling* to move.

"So sweet," he murmured, holding me close against him.

I rest my head against his chest and listened to his pounding heartbeat, counting the beats as it slowed down, only dimly aware of the growing heat around me.

OF COURSE, I'LL STAY

"**H**ow will we get past the next village?" Diek drew a map in the soil, pointing to a square directly in our path. "Go around?"

"Nah," Azrog groaned. "This one's almost a city. It'll add another day to the trip."

Gurm nodded. "But if the humans there see us with Erin, they'll think we kidnapped her."

I chuckled softly. "I'll handle it," I said, waving my fingers in the air. "Let me go on ahead and you'll be able to walk right through the town."

Oruk took my hand in his, holding it close to his chest. "I don't want you in danger. If they try—"

"If they try anything, I can speak to you directly, remember?" I closed my eyes, waiting for his voice.

I don't want to lose you to them, little one.

I smiled, squeezing his hand in reply. *You won't,* I thought back. *My sweet, handsome, magical ogre, how could I want anything else?*

Oruk raised an eyebrow. *It took four of us to please you.*

I laughed, letting go of his hand and pulling my hood around me. Just a quick trip into the tavern should do it—I'd charm enough people to make them think my boys were a traveling circus.

My magic would convince people to look the other way. Their hoods and cloaks would do the rest.

And please me, you do, I replied, giving him a wink and turning back to the road.

"You'll stay?" Oruk called after me.

Of course I'll stay!

DOUBLED BY DWARVES

ᛗᚤᛏᛗᚱᚠᚤᚳᛁᛁᚠᛁᚠᛁᚠᚾᛈᛁᛋᚻᛏᚠᛗᚤᛈᚾᚱᛗᛗᚤᛈᚳᛗᛋᛋᚳᚠᚤᛋᚾᚱᛗ

ZARA JORDAN

THE VOID

ᛗ ᚤ ᛏ ᛗ ᚱ ᚠ ᚤ ᚳ ᛁ ᛙ ᛁ ᚠ ᛁ ᚠ ᚢ ᛈ ᛁ ᚢ ᛏ ᚠ ᛗ ᚤ ᛉ ᚢ ᚱ ᛗ ᛗ ᚤ ᛈ ᛗ ᛗ ᛋ ᛋ ᚳ ᚠ ᚤ ᛋ ᚢ ᚱ ᛗ

I squeezed through a gap between two enormous faces of rock, comforted by the steady drip of water echoing around the cave. The damp stone soaked my fluorescent jacket, the light on my helmet bouncing from every lime-coated surface.

Some people might have found this eerie, but I loved it. Exploring Missouri's caves, I felt like Indiana Jones or Lara Croft. I imagined myself finding some long-lost treasure, or unlocking a cavern of zombies...

Okay, maybe I'll skip the zombies, thanks.

"Amber, wait up!" Ji-ae, my caving partner, called through the narrow gap. "I can't get through there."

"Well, you'd better find another way around, then!" I sing-songed sarcastically.

"Are you serious?" Ji-ae whined. "You're not supposed to go alone."

I rolled my eyes and let out an irritated sigh, safe knowing that Ji-ae couldn't see me. "I'm here now, aren't I? There's a cavern I haven't seen up ahead. I won't be long."

Ji-ae paused, muttering something I couldn't quite catch. Then, her light shone through the narrow gap again. "Fine. I'll see you at the exit. Here—"

They pushed a radio through to me. I took it and tucked the clip into my backpack. "Alright, catch you in a bit."

Secretly, I was glad to get away from Ji-Ae for a while. She didn't have the same sense of adventure as I did, always sticking to the mapped trails blazed before us. I'm not saying she's dull, but...

I picked my way through a narrow stream which had sliced through the rock over thousands of centuries. The stone under my feet was slippery with inch-thick limestone deposits. Stalactites dropped from the ceiling, almost touching their partners on the floor. I weaved around, careful not to damage them.

After only a few yards, the cavern opened up into a large room. Unlike the rest of the cave, the walls here were strangely dimpled, like someone had cut them with hand tools.

"Weird..." I ran my hand along it, noticing how dry it was, and a little warmer. Almost like something was heating it from within, like a geothermal spring.

I pushed in further, aware of the ground underfoot shifting from cold, slippery rock into dusty ground. Well-trodden, and worn away by heavy footfalls.

A rhythmic clanging sound, like metal on stone.

I stopped dead, searching the darkness with my torch. The white beam showed nothing, but as I scanned over the far wall, I noticed a crack where the light wouldn't touch, as if it was being sucked away.

I held my breath and stepped forward, hands outstretched in case I tripped. As I neared the wall, my torch light disappeared—it was like a black hole swallowed it up. On either side of the black void, the cave walls stretched up and behind me, creating the cavernous room. It looked like I was inside a massive stone egg, looking out of a single crack.

I reached for the void, my fingers spreading out as if to touch it.

"Bad idea..." I said under my breath, but my hand kept moving, stretching into the void and through it...

And nothing happened. No pain, no burning, nothing bit my hand off. It was just a gap in the wall. A weird, light-sucking gap, but there was nothing dangerous about it.

Just as I was thinking this, as I wiggled my fingers in the darkness, searching for a surface to touch, something grabbed my wrist and yanked me through the gap into the black void.

I screamed as I fell through the darkness. My torch was useless, my eyes blinded by the lack of light. I could have fallen four feet or four thousand, I couldn't tell you. But it seemed to last forever in slow motion.

I landed with a thump, face down on a rocky cavern floor. A cloud of dust billowed out around me. I pushed myself up on my elbows and saw two pairs of heavy boots pointing at me, illuminated by a flickering orange glow.

"Who the fuck are you?" A gruff man's voice demanded.

I squinted up at the source of his voice, dazzled by the sudden light. "I'm... Amber. Amber Hobbs."

The man gave a snort. "Is that meant to mean something? State your business, Hobbs."

"I don't *have* any business." I struggled to stand, rubbing my eyes to get the dust out of them. "I'm a caver, I was exploring this cavern and—"

When I opened my eyes, I could finally see who stood in front of me.

Well, once I looked down...

I'd fallen into a tunnel—long and winding, with sections on either side that had been mined by hand for metals or gems. Several oil lamps hung from a rope strung along the roof, swaying from a slight gust that traveled through the caves. The metal lanterns squeaked ominously, their glow falling upon the two men in front of me.

Neither were less than four feet tall, short and squat, with broad chests and thick biceps bulging from heavy use. They stood with their chests puffed out, looking like they'd just walked out of a Renaissance Fayre. Leather straps criss-crossed their defined torsos, attaching tool belts and pick axes to their backs. They wore loose cotton pants stained with rock dust and tucked into the tops of their large leather boots.

Both of them had thick reddish beards and long hair—one tied it back in a braid, while the other let it hang in front of his face.

I won't lie. They were kinda hot, despite their small stature. They had a real viking/lumberjack thing going for them.

"What is this?" I grinned. "Dwarf cosplay?"

"*Cosplay*?" The one with floppy hair glared at me. "What're you on about?"

"It's when people dress up as... Never mind. Look, if you could help me get back to the mapped cave systems, that would be great."

"No one *maps* these systems, girl." The other man chuckled dryly. "You either know them, or you die. Now, run along and do either. We've got work to do."

My jaw dropped as they turned away. "You're not just going to *leave* me here? I could get lost, I could *die*."

"Aye, that's what I said!" He didn't turn back. Instead, he hefted a large pickaxe—almost as big as he was—in both hands, and began pounding it against the rock face.

I paused, staring at the muscles in his back as he worked. His shoulders flexed and bulged, and he groaned with the effort of every swing. The sound of his voice, rough and guttural, did something to me, calling to a feral part of me with each grunt.

Nope! No. Nu-uh. You cannot be attracted to the short asshole who told you to fuck off and die.

I cleared my throat. "When I get out of here, I'll report you to the authorities, if you don't help me."

They stopped swinging their picks. In unison, they turned to glare at me.

And they moved like lightning, coming to either side of me so quickly I couldn't catch breath.

The man with braided hair caught me by the wrist and dragged me down to the floor, my knees buckling under me. The other man grabbed my biceps, holding them behind me and pulling me back against his chest.

Braids reached for my chin, lifting for me to look at him.

His icy rage burned into me, making me squirm in his hold.

Sure, they might be short, but they were *strong*. And really, *really* hot. Especially with that look in their eyes.

"Did you just threaten us, girl?" Braids growled at me.

Again, the tone in his voice spoke to some deep, carnal part of me—a part of me that *loved* being commanded in that rough tone.

Oh fuck, what the hell is wrong with you, Amber?

TAKE ME

ᛗ ᛏ ᛏ ᛗ ᚱ ᚠ ᛏ ᚳ ᛁ ᚠ ᛁ ᚠ ᛁ ᚠ ᚾ ᛈ ᛁ ᛋ ᚻ ᛏ ᚠ ᛗ ᛏ ᛉ ᚾ ᚱ ᛗ ᛗ ᛏ ᛈ ᚠ ᛗ ᛋ ᛋ ᚳ ᚠ ᛏ ᛋ ᚾ ᚱ ᛗ

B raids squeezed my chin harder, giving me a meaningful look. "Well?"

I squeaked. "No, I didn't mean it. I'm just... scared. I need to get out of here."

My eyes wandered as I spoke, trailing along Braids' bare chest, covered in a smattering of soft hair across his pecs. A dark line of hair trailed from his bellybutton down into his pants, and I clenched at the thought of pulling them down and finding him hard and ready for me.

When I broke my gaze and looked back at his face, he narrowed his eyes. "Something you like down there?"

I swallowed, shaking my head against his hold.

A ghost of a smile appeared on his face for a moment, before his expression shifted again. He walked away, nodding to the other man. "Doran, tie her up."

"What?" I tried to stand up, but Doran's grip kept me firmly on the ground.

He leaned over my shoulder, tightening his hold on my arms. "Don't move, or it'll be worse for you."

"How could it be worse? You're tying me up! I'm not an animal."

"No," Doran said. "You're a human, and a selfish one at that."

This stunned me so much that I forgot to fight against him. He tied my wrists together with a length of rope.

When he was done, he'd tied my arms up to my elbows, pinned behind my back. He walked in front of me. His bare chest was plastered with tattoos—stylized hammers and anvils swinging across his muscles, throwing black sparks to the other side of his chest. He wrinkled his nose at me, eyeing up my fluorescent clothes. "What *are* you wearing?"

"I could say the same to you." I raised an eyebrow, but softened my features when irritation flickered over his face. "What do you mean 'you're a human', anyway? You're just as human as I am."

Doran spluttered. "*Human*? We're no humans, thank you very much. We're dwarves."

I snorted with laughter, unable to contain it despite my uncomfortable restraints. "Oh, come *on*, pull the other one. Dwarves are fairy tales."

"Doran!" the first man called irritably. "What are you blathering about with her?"

"She's clueless, Kirrick," Doran replied, waving him over. "Thinks dwarves aren't real."

Kirrick strode back to us, swinging his pickaxe over one shoulder as if it weighed nothing. He regarded me coolly, cocking an eyebrow at me before turning to Doran. "Say what, now?"

"Aye, and look at her clothes. I reckon she might be from... you know. That other place."

At Doran's darkly significant tone, Kirrick snapped around to look at me again.

While I was on my knees, he was a little taller than me. He walked around me in a tight circle, examining my clothes, my helmet—which was dangling so loosely it threatened to fall from my head. He reached for the strap under my chin and clicked the fastener, taking it off.

Turning it over in his hands, he gave a curt nod. "Shit."

"What do we do with her?" Doran asked.

"Hello?" I said in my most pissy voice. "Sitting right here, hogtied for your convenience."

Kirrick pointed a finger at me, leaning his face so close to mine, his beard tickled my chin. "Quiet."

A tiny gasp escaped my throat—in part caused by his sharp tone, and partly by the thrill of pleasure that shot straight to my core when he came within kissing distance. He smelled of stone dust and earth mixed with musky *sweat. It* was intoxicating.

He stayed close, still pointing his finger at me. Maybe he'd noticed my weakness.

His proximity made me dizzy, tempting me to lean forward and run my tongue over his lips. My eyes rested on them for much too long, measuring the distance from his face to mine.

Kirrick's mouth twitched into a smirk. "Doran? I reckon she's getting off on this."

"Aye?" Doran came to his side and looked down at my face, lifting my chin with one finger. "You might be right, Kirrick. Not such a fairy tale now, eh, girl?"

Finally finding my voice, I nodded. "Yes, you're both... really hot. But I need to get back."

"Why the rush?" Kirrick smiled. "Before you go, we can teach you a little charity."

"What do you—"

Doran spread his fingers around my throat and squeezed.

I gasped as a spark of pleasure lanced straight to my cunt, throbbing insistently, making me press my thighs together to find some relief.

Doran chuckled. "She's a natural, I reckon. What do you think, girl?"

"A—Amber," I corrected him, knowing that I was pushing a boundary, and not caring. If they'd wanted to hurt me, they'd have already done it. I wanted to see how far this was going to go. Where would they take it? Where would they take *me*?

Doran squeezed my throat a little tighter in response, and the smile fell from his face. "I'll call you what I want to, girl. You understand?"

I nodded, and he released me.

"I'd love to take that pretty mouth of yours," Kirrick said in a low growl.

My chest heaved, my mouth drying at the thought of Kirrick fucking my face with my hands still tied. His biceps twitched, and he licked his lips. I wondered if he was imagining it, too.

They circled me, inspecting me up and down and passing knowing looks to each other.

"What... What are you doing?" I asked.

"Just sizing you up." Kirrick showed me my helmet, turning it around in his hands. "I know how to get you back. But it's a way off, through the caverns."

I glanced at the walls, where I expected to find the black void I'd fallen through. "But there was a gap. Like, a dark gap in the wall."

"Yeah, that's what they say," Doran nodded as they continued circling me. "There are many portals in to this land, but there's only one portal out."

"And that's back at the halls," Kirrick finished.

I waited for them to offer to take me, but they just carried on circling me, tugging at my clothes once in a while, as if inspecting the stitching. Every time the fabric of my coat moved over my skin, it sent another wave of pleasure through me. I closed my eyes and gritted my teeth to stop myself from moaning.

I'd have to ask them. I had to get back, eventually.

"Take me?" I whispered, becoming breathless halfway through at the thought of Kirrick and Doran *taking me* any way they saw fit.

Kirrick smiled—but it was a manic expression, more terrifying than a glare. "What was that, lass?"

Maybe that had come across as more rude than they would have liked. I cleared my throat. "Can you take me to the halls, *please*?"

Doran gave the ropes around my wrists a single pull, and my arms fell free. "That's more like it," he said.

Kirrick handed me my helmet and hoisted his pick over his shoulder with a bright smile. "Follow us, lass."

It was so strange. They were suddenly so calm, so friendly. It was like a dark shadow had lifted from them in an instant.

Stranger still, I wanted that shadow to come back.

SCREAMING TUSTRA

ᛗᛏᛏᛗᚱᚼᛏᚦᛁᚠᛁᚠᛁᚠᚦᛈᛁᛋᚼᛏᚠᛗᛉᛞᚾᚱᛗᛗᛉᛞᚠᛗᛋᛋᛕᚠᛉᛋᚦᚱᛗ

K irrick and Doran led the way down twisting passages, all hewn from the rock, presumably by hand. I couldn't help but keep staring at them—they were perfectly formed, muscles roped along their backs and shoulders, swelling at their necks just enough to make me think of them flexing while they fucked me.

And there was the problem. I wasn't against short guys, per se, but something spectacularly weird was going on here. They weren't dwarves, that was impossible—either they were playing with me for laughs, or I was going insane. Maybe I'd hit my head in the fall.

But the passages seemed real enough. When I reached out to touch them, my fingers trailed against sandy stone, dimpled with shallow cuts.

An image of Kirrick's flexing shoulders flashed in my mind's eye again, morphing into a visual of him flexing that way while he bore down on me. Even his short stature wouldn't overshadow his hefty muscles, his toned abs, the soft hairs on his chest tickling my naked skin...

Oh God, Amber, you really need to speak to someone.

"You alright back there, girl?" Doran called back, smirking at me a little. "Mind wandering off there?"

"A little," I replied, keeping my voice light. "So, where is this place, exactly?"

"You're in the Kingdom of Zetis," Kirrick said. "A mighty hall dug into the mountainside by the dwarves' own hands."

My eyes were glued to his back as he talked, to the pick swaying on his shoulder, his hips flexing as he strode confidently down the winding pathway.

"It's... very cavy." I shook my head. *Pathetic, Amber.*

But they seemed to think it funny, chuckling and shaking their heads. When we came to the end of the tunnel, they halted.

"Take it off," Doran said, pointing at my jacket.

My heart pounded in my ears, not from fear or anger, but sheer excitement. "What?"

Don't argue with him, idiot, just do it!

"There are monsters in these caves, *Tustra,*" Doran said quietly, "and they have excellent eyesight. The lamps go out now, and that jacket gets stowed. It'll be a beacon to the Tustra. I'd like to keep my head today."

My lungs remembered how to work as I unzipped my jacket and handed it to Doran. He stashed it inside a dark leather bag and looked me over.

"That'll have to do. Alright, girl, quietly, now."

The winding passage shifted into a rocky bridge that ascended through a vast cavern. It was so big, the walls and floor dropped out of sight completely, making it appear as though the bridge was passing through an inky void. Soon, it climbed higher, becoming so steep I worried I would fall right off into the black depths below.

I couldn't see any monsters, but I could hear the occasional flapping of wings, the quiet echo of a distant roar. My legs shook as I climbed up behind Doran and Kirrick, who picked along the bridge like it was just a morning stroll.

But they didn't let me fall behind, waiting for me if I stumbled, making sure I kept up with them. I caught the odd eye-roll, though, which made my blood boil. For some reason, I was determined to prove myself to these two strangers.

I was Amber fucking Hobbs. Not some puny little princess who needed saving.

I just needed... a guide, that was all.

When we'd climbed so far up the bridge, my calves burned, the walls of the cavern finally came back into view, as if we'd finally crossed to the other side of an enormous bubble. The bridge pierced the wall a hundred feet in the distance. Kirrick and Doran picked up the pace a little, but kept quiet, their footsteps surprisingly light, for such hefty guys.

They ran the last few steps, beckoning to me to keep up. I picked up my pace, aware of a roar below us, growing louder. The temptation to look behind me grew unbearable, but I pressed on, sure that the moment I saw any monster, it would already be on top of me, jaws wide open and ready to swallow me whole.

The second I reached Kirrick, he clasped my wrist and dragged me towards him, yanking me bodily through the hole in the cavern wall.

He was so strong that I lost my footing, practically flying towards him. He reached around me with both arms, tackling me to the ground just as I heard an ear-splitting shriek above my head.

I craned my neck just in time to see a gigantic gray snake flying through the cavern, screeching as it slithered through the air above the bridge. It rose out of sight, then dive-bombed past the door, descending back into the depths below.

A tiny squeak escaped me as I stared wide-eyed at the space where a giant snake had been—the same space I'd stood a split second before.

"You're okay, girl," Kirrick said softly. "We've got you."

Doran held out his hand to me, and I clasped his wrist, getting to my feet shakily. The moment I stood, my knees gave out beneath me again, and I sank back to the ground.

"You... you saved my life," I said, through gasping breaths.

Kirrick gave me a small smile. "Just didn't fancy seeing you lose your head, is all."

Doran chuckled. "Aye, literally."

They helped me up again and ushered me through a second opening—an archway carved into solid stone. I wasn't sure my legs could carry me any further. The adrenaline was rushing through my system so savagely that I was sure I'd pass out at any moment.

"Just a little further," Doran said, stroking my back—well, practically my ass—comfortingly. "We're almost home."

A TRADE

ᛗᛦᛏᛗᚱᚠᛦᛏᚾᛁᚠᛁᚠᛁᚠᚾᛈᛁᛋᚻᛏᚠᛗᛏᛉᚾᚱᛗᛗᛏᛉᚠᛗᛋᛋᛣᚠᛏᛋᚾᚱᛗ

T he Halls of Zetis were lifted straight out of every fantasy game I'd ever played as a teenager. Stone archways carved with stern faces adorned every hallway, while every hall was vast and cavernous. Kirrick and Doran took me straight to their burrow to recover, promising to take me on to the portal once I'd caught my breath.

Their quarters were smaller than the cavernous halls, but no less impressive—every inch looked like it had been hand-decorated. Geometric patterns and runes covered every inch of the stone, illuminated by a beam of light which bounced around the room using a complex system of mirrors.

Kirrick stretched out on a bench of stone, taking sips from a flask. Doran took the other bench, leaving me trying to choose where to park myself.

Doran patted next to him with a smile, and I perched on the seat, careful to leave a space between us. Since they'd saved me from the Tustra, my heart wouldn't stop pounding in fear. I breathed deeply, trying to calm it.

"You alright there, girl?" Doran reached over to my shoulder and stroked it slowly, rhythmically, both calming me and exciting me all at once.

I moaned low in my chest, closing my eyes and relaxing into his touch. "Yes, thank you. That was... really close."

"Ah, we were *fine*," Kirrick said, handing his flask to me. "That damned Tustra couldn't bite a giant if he saw one."

"I'm really grateful," I said, taking a swig of the sweet liquor. "You didn't have to do that for me."

I swallow, trying to find the courage to say what I so badly wanted to when they had me tied up. *Take me.* "Maybe... maybe I can do something for you both?"

Kirrick glared at me. "What?"

I tried to ignore his anger and placed my hand on Doran's thigh. It was thick and muscular. I felt his muscles twitch at my touch, noticed his jaw clenching. "Something to... to repay you."

Doran grabbed my hand and placed it back on the bench. "Don't," he said glumly.

"We're not monsters, girl," Kirrick growled at me, a fire burning in his eyes. "If we wanted your body in trade, we'd have taken it already."

"I didn't mean it like that—"

"Drop it."

I bit my lip, my eyes finding the floor. I was so sure they'd wanted me, too. And now the burning need that begged for attention would have to go ignored. I pressed my thighs together to relieve the pressure building there, looking anywhere but at Kirrick's or Doran's faces.

"We could teach you a thing or two," Kirrick said without looking at me. "You're only thinking of yourself."

"That's not true!" I said.

Saying nothing, Kirrick stood and moved in front of me. Parting my knees, he stood between them.

I kept my eyes down, too ashamed to look at his face.

"Why do you really want this?" Kirrick asked, tracing a hand from my cheek down my neck. "Is it to thank us? Seems like a stupid reason to fuck someone."

Doran stood too, moving behind me and holding me by my shoulders. "Is it because we're convenient?" he whispered in my ear, the tickling sensation of his breath speaking directly to my cunt. "Willing cocks to use for your own pleasure before you return home? A story to tell your friends over a drink?"

I shook my head, but couln't find the words to deny it. I wasn't thinking of them. I was wondering what it would be like—to fuck a dwarf. Because if the run-in with the Tustra had shown me anything, it was that this was very, very real.

Kirrick lifted my chin, forcing me to look into his eyes. His icy rage burned through me, piercing me from under his heavy eyebrows. "We'll teach you a thing or two about generosity. If you're open to learning, girl."

My mouth hung open for a moment at the thought, my muscles clenching deliciously at their touch. I nodded. "Yes! Yes... please."

Kirrick's frown twisted into a satisfied smirk, and he nodded to Doran, who took a length of rope from his belt.

"Take these off," Kirrick said, plucking at my shirt with his thick forefinger. "And kneel on the floor. Not a word."

My breath came in heavy pants as I did as he told me, lifting the hem of my thin t-shirt and tugging it over my head. I wasn't used to stripping for a man. Usually they did all the work, tearing my clothes off me and worshipping my body while I absorbed the pleasure.

I struggled out of my sports bra with absolutely no grace, and Kirrick raised a hand to his mouth, hiding his growing smirk as he watched.

"Clumsy one, aren't you?" Doran said with a chuckle, taking my hands and spreading them out wide. "Slow down," he said, his eyes raking down my chest, his gaze making my nipples pucker and harden as he watched.

He released me, and I peeled off my pants, slower this time, though still hardly graceful. I stood between them in my thong, breathless and needy.

Doran raised his eyebrows, giving my underwear a pointed look.

I hooked my thumbs under the waistband, but Kirrick's hands rested over mine, stopping me before I could pull them down. He stood close behind me, so I could feel his warm chest pressing against my ass. His breath was shallow and hot on my lower back.

Slowly, achingly slowly, he moved my hands down my legs, so I had to bend over double as he pushed my hands lower. The further he went, the more my butt pressed into him, until I could feel his beard tickling my thighs.

When my hands reached my ankles, he held them there, nuzzling my ass. Then he ran his nose along my sex, inhaling deeply.

"Oh, my god..." I shuddered, burning with shame at his lewd treatment, but loving it at the same time.

Doran stepped closer, running the rope through his hands. "Stay still," he said, his voice husky with desire. He tied my hands behind my back, knotting the restraints right up to the elbow again.

A little tug on the rope, and he had me standing upright again, stepping out of my underwear. Doran pulled me around the room a little, giving me orders to turn, to lean forward. Then he brought me back to the stone bench.

"Bend over," he said, nodding his head to the back of the bench.

SELFLESS

ᛗᛏᛏᛗᚱᚠᛏᚇᛁᚠᛁᚠᛁᚠᚇᛔᛁᛋᚻᛏᚠᛗᛏᛗᛚᚱᛗᛗᛏᛗᚱᛗᛋᛋᚒᚱᛏᛋᚇᚱᛗ

I bent double, folding forward over the backrest with my hands tight behind my back. It amazed me how calm I felt—I knew I would do anything they asked me to. My sex throbbed as my imagination ran wild. What would they have me do next? I lifted my head and stared right at Kirrick's erect cock, thick-shafted with a huge, bulbous head. He stroked it deliberately, grinning down at me.

"You're going to satisfy us, girl," Kirrick said in a hoarse voice. "We'll take it in turns with you, and the only reward you'll have is the pleasure of making us come. Understand?"

I nodded, my mouth watering at the sight of his cock waiting before me.

"Open your mouth," Kirrick said, gripping the back of my head.

I did as I was told, licking my lips and opening my mouth wide as he pushed inside, sliding over my tongue and easing to the back of my throat. He let out a long hiss of pleasure, shaking as he restrained himself, thrusting into my mouth with such aching slowness that I began to wish he would fuck my face, like he had in my imagination.

I kept my eyes open, watching the pleasure on his face—the way his cheeks twitched when he touched the back of my throat, the sounds he made, his fingers clutching at my hair and pulling me on to him.

Soon, I noticed the desire in my cunt had intensified, burning even hotter at the sight of Kirrick losing himself in me.

Behind me, Doran stroked my legs, teasing me with small circles, inching ever closer between my thighs until I hummed low in my throat, begging him to put me out of my misery. Every time I made a noise, though, he moved away, leaving me aching and begging for more attention. Only when the sensation subsided did he start the torture again, making the smooth circles with his thumbs, moving in towards my cunt, stopping, then moving back to my ass.

A small whimper of frustration escaped me.

Doran lifted his hand and smacked me playfully on my ass cheek. "Patience," he said calmly. "This isn't for your pleasure, girl."

Oh, but how wrong he was. With every thrust of Kirrick's cock, my orgasm hovered within reach, making me dizzy with need.

I willed him to go harder, to fuck my face, to come inside me. I wanted to beg Doran to fuck me, too, to stop the endless torture of my thighs. But they continued, slowing whenever I neared my orgasm, and picking up the speed until I was raw from them.

Kirrick growled, clutching my hair and pushing deeper into my throat. I mewled in bliss as he finally picked up speed, his biceps flexing. I focused on his face, his mouth curling into a grimace of aggressive lust, his chest tensing from the effort of restraining himself.

He groaned with pleasure and stilled, his hot cum coating the back of my tongue. I swallowed, savoring his musky, salty tang. He pulled away, leaving me cold and still teetering on the brink of orgasm.

I wanted to complain, but the moment I opened my mouth, Doran had taken his place. He took the same position, guiding my mouth to his hard cock, a thick vein bulging along the shaft, a drop of dew at the tip. I took him in willingly, wiggling my hips and writhing against the bench, hoping to find some release.

"No, you don't." Doran grabbed my tied hands and pressed me deeper into the bench, so it became difficult to breathe. He pulsed his hips, fucking my face, using just the right pressure to keep me pinned while keeping his hands free to hold me down.

Behind me, Kirrick spread my ass cheeks wide apart, baring my pussy to the cold air. I groaned as he blew on me, his hot breath burning over my clit.

"You need more, girl?"

With my mouth stuffed full of Doran, it was impossible to answer. I gave him a muffled 'mm-hmm' in the vain hope that he'd take pity on me.

In an instant, his mouth was on me, suckling at my clit and lapping my juices. I squealed with the bliss of it, making Doran grunt from the vibration on his cock. He pulled out of my mouth, lifting me up and pushing his balls into my face. "Suck," he said, and I opened wide, sucking on his ballsack with relish.

Kirrick growled into my pussy, biting down gently on my clit. I ground against his face, desperate to reach my own climax, but the moment I tried, he moved away, leaving me aching and wanting.

I sobbed, but Doran gripped my hands tighter, pulling my arms back so that they twisted awkwardly.

"I haven't had my fill of you yet," he grumbled. "You get to come when I've spilled my load all over your tits."

My eyes rolled, but I relaxed into his hold, letting my weight hang from the ropes. He seemed happy at this and gave Kirrick a curt nod over my shoulder.

In seconds, Kirrick's mouth was back at my pussy, licking, sucking, nibbling at my clit.

Doran pumped his cock in one hand while I licked and sucked on his balls, his gaze flicking to my chest repeatedly. He pulled me up to a standing position, pumping his cock frantically until his cum shot out in thick ropes, coating my tits.

Kirrick backed away, too, circling my clit with his thumb before sliding it inside me. I leaned back against the heel of his hand and shuddered.

"Good," he said breathlessly. "How was that?"

"So good," I groaned.

"What was good about it?" Kirrick asked, his voice husky.

"Watching you, seeing you enjoy me—" I sucked in a shaking breath. "—I got so turned on just by watching you come."

Doran grinned, and hauled me over to a bed—also made of stone, but covered in thick furs and woolen blankets. He lay me down and crawled in behind me, pulling me between his legs.

Kirrick climbed on the bed after us, stroking his cock and smiling down at me. "How badly do you want us, Amber?"

I gasped at the sound of my name on his lips, my cunt burning with need. "Please," I moaned, "take me. I'll do anything."

Kirrick grinned, climbing on top of me so I was sandwiched between them, and pressing the head of his thick cock at my entrance. I tried tilting my hips towards him, but Doran held me still. Kirrick kept his eyes locked on mine as he pressed forward, inching inside me, taking me, making me tremble with desire.

Doran reached around me, cupping my breasts and teasing my nipples until jolts of pleasure streaked down my body. I gasped, bucking against Kirrick as he sank in right to the hilt, hissing his satisfaction between his teeth.

He gripped me by the hips and lifted me, still inside me, switching our positions so I was on top of him.

"Now," he said. "*Now* you take what you need."

I couldn't wait any longer. It was difficult to keep my balance, with my hands still tied, but I rocked my hips, grinding my clit against Kirrick's pelvic bone, relishing the feel of his thick thighs beneath me. Being so much larger than him, taller and longer-legged, made my core work overtime to hold position, but the pressure of his pelvic bone against my clit hit just right, making my thighs tense.

Doran wrapped his arms around me from behind, bending me forward again and pressing his cock against my ass. "Will you take both of us, Amber?"

I sighed, desperate to know how it felt. I'd had anal sex before, but never with two guys inside me at once. "Yes," I breathed. "Please."

Doran pushed inside, stretching me until I shivered from the overload of sensations flooding me.

We moved as one, rocking and grinding on each other until my ears buzzed with my own heartbeat. I released a high pitch of agony as they pushed deeper inside me, sharing me.

Warmth flooded my body, covering every inch of my skin. Every muscle tensed as the pleasure reached its apex, crashing over me like a tidal wave.

No one ever made me come like that before, that whole-body orgasm that seemed to stretch out forever, intensifying the more I thought about it. They had spent so long priming me for it, teasing me, denying me, that when it finally came, I reveled in it, basking in the sunshine and absorbing every sensation.

When we finally came down together, we collapsed in a heap, completely spent. Doran untied my arms and grabbed a blanket from the bottom of the bed and covered me up, murmuring something about the cold, but I was too far gone, already drifting into a deep, exhausted sleep.

TAKE A RISK

ᛗ ᚤ ᛏ ᛗᚱ ᚠ ᚤ ᚲᛁᚠ ᛁ ᚠ ᛁ ᚠ ᚢᚠ ᛁ ᛋ ᚺ ᛏ ᚠ ᛗ ᚤ ᛗᚢᚱ ᛗ ᛗ ᚤ ᛗ ᚠ ᛗ ᛋ ᛋ ᚲ ᚠ ᚤ ᛋ ᚢᚱ ᛗ

T he portal looked exactly how I expected it to. A big, wibbly
    wobbly thing in mid-air, surrounded by stone carvings and
runes and all kinds of magical-looking shit.

But no matter how much I wanted to go home, I couldn't bring
myself to walk through it.

Doran and Kirrick stood on either side of me, guarding me while I
stared at the magical doorway that would take me home.

"What if I don't go?" I blurted out.

Kirrick's eyebrows nearly rose to the ceiling. "What do you mean,
'not go'? That's your home."

"I know…" I glanced back at the portal, but still felt something
keeping me here, tugging on me like an invisible tether. "But just say,
for instance, I didn't go. Could I do anything here?"

"Like what?" Doran asked shrewdly.

"Like… work. A job. Some way of earning a place here. It's… pretty
cool, you know? Giant flying snakes aside…"

Kirrick chuckled. "Go, Amber. There's nothing for you here."

I frowned, surprised by how much that hurt.

"Don't get me wrong," he continued, apparently picking up on my
reaction. "I'd keep you here, if I could—"

"But it won't last," Doran finished, his expression glum. "You'd want to go back, eventually. It's where you belong."

"Alright," I said, glancing about the vast hall of stone. "You might be right. But do I have to go back right away?"

Kirrick frowned.

"She could stay a little while longer, Kirrick," Doran said, stroking my thigh gently, stirring my desire.

"Aye," Kirrick said, glancing around at the other dwarves. Some eyed me suspiciously. Some, I couldn't help but notice, looked me up and down hungrily. Kirrick gave them a menacing stare. "But not in the halls."

"Where else could we go?" I asked hopefully.

Doran shrugged. "How about we work that out later, too?"

I took a pen and paper from my pack, and scribbled a hasty note to Ji-ae, before tucking it under the clip of the radio. Stepping right up to the portal, I glanced back at Doran and Kirrick. "So, if I throw this through, it should go to where I left the caves?"

They nodded, watching the note in my hand and sharing curious glances.

"Alright, then." I took the radio and hurled it through the shining light.

• • • •**•**• **•** • •

Ji-ae

I'm sorry. I shouldn't have abandoned you. I was selfish. I hope you found a safe path through the caves.

I don't know if you'll ever find this letter, or when I'll come back. But please don't waste your time looking for me—I'm safe, and healthy, and I'll find my way home some day.

Just do one thing for me?

Take a risk, once in a while. Just a little one.

Amber x

EXPOSED BY THE FAE

ZARA JORDAN

A TRIO OF SCOTS

Friday night in The Drunken Scot was busy as ever, and by that I mean it was dead. We had the usual crowd, mostly, except for the group of three men in the corner booth, huddled together and laughing raucously over some funny story.

While I pulled pints for our sparse customers, I found my gaze drifting over to their table, more than once. They were such a rag-tag bunch, an odd assortment to see out drinking together.

You get used to how people cluster when you work behind a bar. It's rare to see a group of friends who don't look like each other in some way—in their style, or their behavior. But these three were as different from each other—and everyone around them—as you could get.

I'd learned their names over the course of the evening. Between me and Judith, we'd discovered that they were here on holiday from Scotland, and the first job on their list was to find a Scottish Bar. Check.

"Reckon they're ready for another round?" Judith nudged me with her hip, nodding at their booth.

"My turn!" I stepped back from the bar, wiping my hands and clipping the handheld to my apron.

Judith rolled her eyes. "Fine. But I want all the info you get on them! Plenty of them to share."

Yeah... right, I thought with a smirk.

As I passed the wall-length mirror at the end of the bar, I gave my reflection a quick glance—clean white shirt, tucked in, nothing on my face, no panty lines. I wiped away a small smudge of mascara from the corner of my eye and tucked a stray hair behind my ear. One day, I promised myself to let it stay natural, embrace the afro. For now, I had to learn to like what I saw looking back at me.

Okay, now think of something funny.

I channeled the flirtatious energy I'd tucked away earlier in the day, putting on a smile and sauntering over to the Scots' table.

"Boys," I leaned over them, much closer than necessary, before correcting myself and standing more formally. My cheeks burned as they turned to regard me all at the same time. "Can I get you a fresh one?"

"Ah, you don't have tae be embarrassed, Karlee," Carson—the rugged redhead—drawled in his thick accent. "If ya wanna get close, we'll make a space." He patted the seat next to him, making my cheeks burn even hotter.

"Yeah," Lucas—the latino with a gorgeous sleeve of tattoos on his left arm—joined in. "Or if the seat's full, there's always our laps."

"Lucas!" Taylor—the musician with designer stubble and hands I couldn't stop staring at—swatted Lucas on the shoulder with a grin. "She's a lady, ya can't go propositioning every woman like that."

Lucas grunted. "Wouldn't say it to any woman..."

"Uh—" I waved a hand at their drinks, unable to form words. "—did you have... an order?"

Dammit Karlee, what the hell is wrong with you? They're hot, and they're flirting with you—flirt back!

As soon as this thought crossed my mind, all three men turned to look at me again before sharing a look. It was unnerving—as if they'd literally heard my thoughts.

"Alright," Carson said, holding up his hands. "We'll have three pints o' heavy, lass."

"And three drams of whisky," Taylor continued. "Your recommendation."

With this, he pointed at me with a grin. My eyes trained directly to his fingers—long and tapered, with perfectly trimmed nails and just a small smattering of soft, downy hair at his wrist. An image of his knuckles sinking inside me flashed across my mind.

Shit!

Taylor grinned.

"O-Okay—" I tapped their order into the handheld, too afraid to look in their eyes any more. "Coming right up."

"Hey, Karlee—" Lucas called as I turned away, desperate to hide my shame. I turned back to them slowly, my eyes still trained on the floor. "Make sure you bring the drinks to us, yeah? We have something to ask you."

· · · · ●· ● ● · ·

"That's it!" Judith clapped her hands in mock irritation. "Oh, I'm so angry with you, Karlee. You couldn't even let me have one of them?"

"I didn't say anything, I swear!" I replied, arranging the glasses neatly on my tray. "I can barely get a word in. They're too—"

"Hot? Sexy? Smoldering?" She batted her eyelashes.

"Yes. But also... insightful, I guess? It's like they know what I'm thinking."

Judith laughed. "Well, of course, silly. It's written all over your face. And theirs. They haven't taken their eyes off you." She motioned to the Scots' table, where all three men watched me—me—without saying a word.

The relaxed smirks on their faces, and the way their eyes trailed over my body as I stood at the bar, spoke volumes.

"Help." I grabbed Judith's wrist. "Help me. I can't do this. You know how useless I am at this stuff, Jude."

"Yup! And there's no better time to learn than the present, sunshine." She beamed at me, placing the last pint on my tray with a wink. "Break a leg."

"Oh, God..." I lifted the tray and fight hard to stop shaking. *Come on, Karlee. You can make it. Just get to their table without spilling anything, and get away. You can't handle this. It's too much. Just get your pay packet, get home, and by next week, you can book a handyman. This shower needs fixing, stat! Do not think about the sexy men. Don't think about them kissing your neck, or stroking your thighs... Shit!*

I stopped short just before colliding with a broad chest in a blue cotton shirt. Tilting my head up, I looked into Carson's warm amber eyes, and he smirked back, holding on to the tray gently to stop it from spilling. "Mind elsewhere, lass?"

I gave a nervous laugh, gripping the tray even as he tried to take it away from me. "Oh God I'm so sorry—"

"Please," Carson waved a hand with a smile, dismissing my apologies. "Let me help you with that."

Taylor raised a hand. "And maybe we can all help you with—"

Lucas elbowed him in the stomach, cutting him off mid-sentence.

Carson set the glasses on the table, talking me down every time I tried to do it myself. Once the drinks were set on the table top, he gave a pointed look at the clock overhead. "Is your shift nearly over?"

I frowned. "Yes, actually. I get off around ten."

Taylor opened his mouth, but closed it again on a cold look from Lucas. My cheeks burned hot again—it felt like I was always blushing around these guys.

"Can we give you a tip?" Carson reached into his pocket.

"Oh no, please, there's no need—" I raised a hand to stop him, and my fingers brushed against his wrist. The momentary skin contact wiped my mind clean of all thought and replaced it with an instant burning need—like I was on the verge of an intense orgasm.

My knees buckled and I landed heavily. Lucas had moved the chair just in time to stop my fall. His hand rested on my shoulder, easing me back against the backrest. "You okay?"

"There's... really no need," I panted, wondering where this sudden faintness had come from. "There's a pot on the bar... we all share it."

"Please," Carson pushed a rolled up note into my hand, closing my fingers around it. "Maybe you can fix that shower."

He winked, and somehow, even through the heady fog of desire clouding my thoughts, realization dawned crystal-clear. "You're fae!"

A DEBT UNPAID

Taylor grinned. "How did you know?"

The Fae were a rarity in New York—they preferred to live in greener spaces—but I'd heard enough about them to wonder if I'd ever have the chance to meet one. They were mind-readers, and gifted with nature magic, among other things... I'd heard all about them from my grandmother. Nature wasn't the only magic under their control, either—according to her stories, they were romantic creatures who seduced anyone they touched.

"My grama grew up in Carolina. She told me about a fae friend she had as a child."

"And you believed her?" Taylor raised his eyebrows. "Most people would brush that off as bullshit."

I stared at my hand where Carson had touched me. The skin still tingled, leaving a warm shiver of lust. "I wasn't ever exactly... sure. But she said they looked different. Shimmery, kinda..."

They grinned. "It's a glamor," Lucas said, holding his hand up. "Magic, to help us blend in."

With that, his hand changed color, from tawny brown to a dark purple, covered in tiny shimmering lights. Then, as quickly as it had faded, it returned to normal.

"Well, now that's out of the way..." Carson took the seat next to me so I was trapped in the booth with them, stuck between him and Lucas. "Would ya like to talk some more about those delicious thoughts of yours, lass?"

Beneath the table, his fingers brushed my thigh. A small moan bubbled up in my throat. I swallowed it back, glancing at Judith in what I hoped was a signal for help. She gave me two thumbs up and continued serving.

Gee, thanks, Jude.

"I didn't mean any harm—" a small gasp escaped me as Lucas stroked my other thigh, his finger rhythmically moving back and forth. "—It's not like I knew you could hear my thoughts..."

"No, that's true." Taylor leaned his elbows on the table, steepling his hands and gazing at me intently over his fingers. Those fingers...

Damn, he really does know.

Taylor grinned. "We haven't taken offense, Karlee, don't panic. We have a proposition for you."

My heart fluttered against my ribs. "M-Me? What could the fae want with me?"

"You said about your nan," Carson's warmth radiated from him, or maybe it was my blood getting hot under their attentive gaze. "It turns out the Seely court owes her a favor. And our job involves repaying the court's debts."

"The Seely... what?"

"A Fae organisation," Taylor explained. "Karlee, I'm going to be frank with you. The Seely don't enjoy being in anyone's debt."

"But my grandmother's—"

"We know," Lucas said, pulling away from me. I appreciated the show of respect for my late grandmother, but I wanted him back. I already felt cold without him leaning in to me. "But the debt doesn't go away. Our family owes your family."

"What did she do?"

Carson followed Lucas' lead and sat up straight. They looked grave, bowing their heads in respect as he explained.

"Your nan saved one of our leaders back in the sixties. They were going to be taken back to... well, away." A dark look passed over his face. "But she vouched for them, gave them a safe haven. She never called in her debt."

I smiled. "Sounds just like grama." She wouldn't have asked for them to repay her, not for something as small as that. Hospitality was second nature to my grama—she wouldn't have seen it as a service that needed repaying.

"Well, regardless," Taylor's hands flexed and his eyes met mine, "the debt is unpaid. We have to clear the balance. And your grandmother's services were significant."

"Really, she would have been fine with this," I glanced at Judith again, half hoping that she'd be irritated with me for taking so long, rushed off her feet. Instead, I found her leaning against the bar, playing on her phone with no one left to serve. Dammit.

"She fed every kid on the street when I was growing up," I continued with a smile. "This wouldn't have been any different to her."

Carson stroked my thigh again, higher this time, so his thumb grazed near my panty-line. "Please, Karlee," he said. "Don't shake this off. Let us do this for you."

"We can give you everything you want," Taylor said. "Everything."

I wanted to say yes, with every fiber of my being, but I couldn't shake the feeling that I was being paid back for something I'd had no part in. The doubts in the back of my mind stopped me from saying the words, but judging by the warm, sexy smiles that broke out on all their faces at once, it was obvious they were poking about in my mind again.

I opened my mouth to speak, feeling like all the air had been sucked out of the room. "I—"

"Just coming over to let you off the hook," Judith interrupted, putting one hand on her hip and motioning to the table. "It's dead tonight. Go have fun."

Carson, Lucas and Taylor all turned to her, still flashing their charm like lighthouse beams. Judith froze, doe-eyed under their gazes. "Uh, unless there's something else I can get you?"

Taylor smiled, talking casually to her even as Carson and Lucas continued stroking my thighs under the table. My breathing became shallow, my pulse thrumming in my neck so hard I swore everyone could hear it. Somewhere on the edge of my attention, I heard Taylor dismissing Jude, thanking her and handing her another tip.

"Come for us, Karlee," Carson whispered in my ear.

My mouth popped open, sure I'd misheard him. Surely he'd said 'Come with us.'

Carson grinned, staring me dead in the eye as he shook his head slowly.

· · · ● · ● ● ● · ·

The soaked streets reflected bar signs and billboards from overhead. Carson and Lucas walked in front, casually joking about some friends back home, while Taylor walked by my side, guarding me from the street in a casually chivalrous way.

We'd only walked two blocks when he pointed to a side road. "That one?"

My breath caught in my throat, but I nodded, pressing my lips together. How was I possibly going to go through with this? Out here, practically in the middle of the street?

Carson and Lucas led the way, ducking into the side street and checking every darkened corner.

It was just a small side alley, dark and damp with a fire escape that snaked up the side of a brick apartment building. But some dark part of me had always had a fantasy about this dark and possibly dangerous place... one that I could never say out loud.

Halfway along the alley, Taylor caught my wrist and pulled me back against him, pressing the length of his body along mine. From first appearances, he'd almost seemed tall and lanky—I hadn't paid attention to much more of him than his hands. But now I felt how hard his body was against mine. His hand circled both my wrists with ease, and he pulled my hands down to his crotch, where I felt his erection pressing against his jeans.

I gasped, shocked at how sudden it all was.

But it wasn't sudden at all. It felt that way, because I hadn't asked for it. I hadn't told them what I wanted.

They just... knew.

And now, Carson and Lucas faced me, watching us and licking their lips, eyeing me up and down with the same hungry look they'd given me in the bar.

"You know, we're not just doing this because of a debt, Karlee," Carson said.

"We talked all night," Lucas said. "About how lucky we were to be chosen for this job."

Taylor pulled my hands closer to him, pushing his swollen bulge against my palms. "See what you're doing to us, Karlee? How much we want you?"

I groaned, leaning back against him while Carson reached for my shirt, pulling it out of my pants and bunching it up over my lacy bra. A thrill rushed through me as a rush of cool air traced my skin, puckering my nipples.

Carson sighed his appreciation, leaning in to nuzzle my breasts. His beard tickled me, making me squirm against Taylor's firm hold.

Fuck, that feels so good...

Still, I *wanted* to tell them what to do, to tell them where and how I imagined them fucking me, that I wanted them all at once, filling every hole, or sharing me, taking turns. I opened my mouth and imagined saying the words, telling them every explicit detail in a sexy, low voice.

But nothing came out.

"Don't worry, love," Lucas weaved his fingers around the back of my head, through my hair—gently at first, then pulling slightly, tugging backwards so I looked up into his warm brown eyes. His lips were so close to mine, they brushed together as he spoke. "If you can't say it, just think it. We want to please you. In fact, we can't fucking wait."

He pulled me towards him and kissed me, controlling me with one hand, claiming me—kissing me so hard it felt like I'd have bruises on my lips when he was done with me.

Carson tugged at my bra, releasing one of my breasts and taking my nipple in his mouth. The warmth of his tongue after the cold night air sent a shiver of excitement down my back, where Taylor unzipped his pants with his free hand.

He slid his cock into my palm, still gripping me by the wrists, using me to jack him off.

Fuck, this is hot.

Just at the end of the street, New York nightlife bustled about, oblivious to the four degenerates getting off on each other down a quiet alleyway. I wondered what would happen if somebody caught us, walked over to us. Would they stop or make them watch?

"I'd fuck you on their lap if you wanted me to, Karlee," Taylor grunted into my ear, flexing his hips to push his thick cock back and forth between my fingers. "Tie them up and take you right on top of them."

I moaned into Lucas's mouth at the thought.

"Maybe we should find an audience, then?" Carson mumbled against my tits, pinching my other nipple and tugging it mercilessly, sending streaks of pleasure-pain straight to my clit. "I know a few places..."

I sank against them, absorbing the sensations, opening wider to Lucas's probing tongue.

"Just down this way!" A strange voice broke the spell, making me freeze in shock. What had felt like a sexy idea now became a reality, and fear quickly replaced every ounce of lust in me.

No, I can't.

Instantly, all three men backed off without a word. Carson pulled my shirt down, gently tucking it into the front of my pants without a single smirk. Taylor zipped up, steadying my weight but freeing my hands. Lucas broke our kiss, releasing my head from his grasp and turning to speak to the strangers coming down the alley.

"Hey, I think we're lost. How far are we from East 39th?"

SEELY COURT REQUEST LINE

They walked me right back to my doorstep, no matter how many times I told them I was fine. They were only satisfied when I opened the lobby and showed my name on the buzzer list.

"Hey," I murmured, too awkward to look any of them in the eye. "I'm really sorry about—"

"Uh-uh," Taylor said, patting my shoulder. "There's nothing to be sorry about."

"But we do still have that debt to pay," Carson said, taking my hand and kissing my knuckles.

As he released me, he slipped a card into my palm. I turned it over, frowning at the numbers embossed in gold. "An international number?"

"That goes direct to the Seely Court," Lucas said. "It's a request line."

"Call that number and tell them anything you really want." Carson said. "Anything, it'll be yours. Then, our debt will be paid."

· · · ● ·● · ● · · ·

There was no way in hell I was going to get to sleep that night. Alone in my apartment, I stayed awake right through till morning, turning over the events from the night in my mind. What would have happened if I hadn't said no? Would they really have fucked me in the alley?

Would that have been such a bad thing?

Taylor had even said he'd tie someone up and fuck me on their lap... That couldn't be true...

But they did say people could ask for anything. What kind of debts had they already repaid?

I shuddered at the dark turn my thoughts took.

The business card sat on my nightstand. I picked it up for the umpteenth time and stared at the numbers—a quick search online had revealed it was a British number, somewhere in Scotland—because of course.

"Call that number and tell them anything you really want."

But I didn't really want anything. Sure, I was working towards a nicer home, maybe a better career in the future. But these weren't things I wanted given to me on a plate—much less for a debt owed to someone else. I wanted my achievements to be my own, and that was the end of it.

I glanced at my bathroom door and bit my lip. I guess I could ask for help fixing my shower...

That was on par with what Grama had done, right? A favor for a favor. It seemed much more fair than the kinds of favors those three sexy Scots had been suggesting.

The second I'd even had an inkling of doubt, they'd backed off. Not one of them had made another lewd comment or looked at me with anything other than concern, or a friendly smile. They were gentlemen to the last moment.

It was such a flipped switch from how they'd acted in the alley... they were practically animals, all over me...

I picked up my mobile and dialed the number, double-checking every digit of the unfamiliar pattern. The call took a little longer than usual to connect, but then rang. Once, twice...

"Hello and welcome to the Seely Court request line." A female voice in a heavy Scottish accent sing-songed. "Your message is treated in the strictest of confidence. This is a direct line to debt settlement group three, who will take your request at their earliest convenience. Please leave your name and your request after the tone."

The line beeped, and I opened my mouth, took a deep breath, and hung up.

"No." I slipped the card back into my nightstand drawer and flopped back on my bed, hugging my pillow and screwing my eyes shut. "Just think about it in the morning, Karlee."

· · • • • • • • · ·

"So, how did it go?" Judith waggled her eyebrows at me the moment I walked through the door for our Saturday shift.

"Ugh, it didn't." I rolled my eyes. "Usual shit, different day."

"Karlee!" Jude slapped her forehead so loud the sound rung around the empty bar. "You had them in the palm of your hand, girl!"

A memory of Taylor's cock sliding through my hand made me blush. *Oh, you have no idea.*

"I know. But I just... couldn't go through with it."

"Well, shit. What a waste." Judith made a sympathetic face and pulled me in for a hug. "Next time, I'm gonna buy you a male hooker."

I laughed, hugging her back. "Jude..."

"I mean it, Karlee. We gotta get you out of this slump!"

"If you had your way, I'd be sleeping my way through every apartment in New York."

"Not every apartment. Only about half. I'd take the other half." She winked.

Our shift picked up quickly, with more customers passing through the bar than the night before. More than once, I thought I saw a flash of red hair, a tattooed arm, or those fingers... but by the time I turned to look, there was either no one there at all, or someone completely different.

During the rare quiet moments, my mind wandered back to the business card on my nightstand. I wondered what fantasy I could ask for, and whether I could ask for those three to satisfy it. I had so many fantasies that I'd never dared to tell a man. Hell, I'd never spoken them out loud at all, even to Judith, and I told her almost everything about my lacking love life.

All night, I kept hoping the trio would come back to the bar so I could ask them... questions. I didn't even know how to put my reservations into words. It just felt wrong, like I was forcing them to do something against their will.

"We want to please you. In fact, we can't fucking wait."

I remembered the feel of Lucas' lips on mine. No, I hadn't forced them to do anything. They could have just as easily picked up on my issues with my shower and offered to fix that in repayment. Instead, they picked out my horny fantasies and indulged them without question.

It was almost like they got off on it as much as I did...

On the way home, I took out my mobile and scrolled through my call list. Scotland's number was right there, waiting for me to dial. My finger hovered over the list...

But what will you even ask for? You haven't made your mind up, yet.

"The shower," I told myself. "I'll just ask for someone to come fix my shower. It'll be fine."

I tapped the contact and waited for the line to connect, picking up the pace along the abandoned sidewalks. One ring, two...

"Hello and welcome to the Seely Court request line..."

I waited for the message to play out, rehearsing my message in my head again and again.

Hello, my name is Karlee Garner. I'd like to have my shower fixed. Thank you.

Hello, my name is Karlee Garner. I'd like to have my shower fixed. Thank you.

The line beeped loudly. I cleared my throat. "Hello, my name is Karlee Garner. I'd like to be fucked in public by Carson, Lucas and Taylor."

My mouth popped open like a goldfish out of water. I let out a small choked sound and hung up the phone.

What the fuck???

A couple walking towards me gave me a wide berth, side-eyeing me as if I was contagious. Realizing I was still out in the streets, I tucked my phone away and headed for home, staring at my feet hitting the sidewalk.

The moment I'd started talking, the words just spilled from me automatically, like they were being pulled from me. And yeah, okay, maybe I did want to get railed by the three hot Scottish dudes, but I was Karlee Garner—I didn't just say that shit out loud!

But it was okay—they couldn't take that seriously. They'd put it down to a drunk call, or a prank. There's no way they'd act on that request.

No way.

"Well hey there, Karlee." A familiar accent, a deep Scottish voice with a hint of rasp.

The three pairs of boots in front of me stood still, like they were waiting for me to look up.

I gulped, despite the flutter of excitement that ran through me. "Oh, shit."

THE ROOF

"Mind if we walk you home?" Taylor asked, a smirk twitching at the corner of his lip. "Or did you mean a different Carson, Lucas and Taylor?"

I squared my shoulders and adopted an air of confidence. "No, I meant to ask for you to fix my shower, actually."

They fell into step beside me, none making any effort to hide their amusement. Then Carson slapped a hand to his forehead.

"Oh, I might have forgotten to mention—" he grinned "—the Seely request line is enchanted."

I stopped walking, oblivious to the sparse strangers passing us on the sidewalk. "What?"

"Yeah," Lucas joined in, "it will only let you say what you *really* want."

A small squeak escaped me.

"So," Carson said, leaning in to me and stroking my shoulder. "Where shall we go?"

"I... I don't know." It felt like they could see right through me. Like there was no way of hiding the burning heat between my thighs, how my breathing had sped up, my heart pounding against my ribcage, trying desperately to get out.

"Karlee." Taylor put two fingers under my chin and made me look up into his eyes. "We won't make you do anything you don't want to. But you can't expect people to read your mind all the time. So why don't you look at this as practice, training, even?"

"Training?"

"We already know you want this. Try asking for it."

My knees practically buckled beneath me at the thought. Even though they already knew what I was going to say, the thought of this being some elaborate trap still hovered in my imagination. I swallowed the dry lump in my throat and nodded. "Oh, okay. Uh. I'd like—"

They waited patiently, raising their eyebrows.

"—uh, that is..."

"Out with it, Karlee." Lucas touched my elbow.

"Fuck me in the alley," I blurted out before clapping a hand to my face. Here it comes. This is when they all point, and laugh, and tell you how fucked up you are.

"We'd love to," Carson drawled.

The panicked butterflies in my stomach disappeared. I relaxed, letting my hands drop back to my sides. "Really?"

"Really."

"But maybe not the alley." Lucas said, glancing at the people passing us. "We have a place in mind, if you're open to it?"

I nodded, trying to contain my sudden excitement.

They led me another block away, down a back street. A tall brick apartment, similar to my own. The block hummed with quiet activity—music from windows, murmurs of conversation. We stopped at the bottom of the fire escape that trailed up the side of the building.

Carson went first, followed closely by Lucas. Taylor touched my elbow and leaned in close. "If you have any doubts, you only need to say the word. Or even think it. We'll back off, just like last time. Okay?"

I nodded again, trying to find the words to thank him.

"No need to thank me. I'm looking forward to this as much as you are, Karlee." He grabbed my ass and squeezed, groaning low in his throat. "I can't wait to feel you on my cock."

I leaned against his hand, enjoying the firm grip of his fingers on my ass, and closed my eyes. "I can't wait either," I said, surprised at how easy it was. Feeling brave, I ventured further. "Jacking you off wasn't enough."

Taylor trailed kisses along my shoulder, nipping gently at my neck with a low growl. "Then we should hurry up," he said, smacking my ass.

I grinned and followed the others, practically running up the steps despite my weak knees. We climbed past one floor after the other, hissing at each other to be quiet when we passed a window with a light on, giggling like drunk teenagers. At the top of the building, the fire escape joined on to the roof—an expanse of concrete, nothing special, but around us, I could see the whole of Greenwich Village lit up, and a low hum of activity rose to meet us.

The second I stepped on the concrete, Carson was on me, wrapping his hands around my waist and kissing my neck.

"Ah!" I dropped my purse and draped my arms around his neck. Eager to find some release, I pressed up against him, satisfied by the large bulge in his jeans.

Behind me, Lucas kissed the other side of my neck, squeezing my hips and grinding against my ass. It was like being fed from by vampires, but instead of draining me, they filled me with more energy, more need, more desire. But they didn't need to go slow—I was ready, more than ready, I was desperate. I wanted to feel them inside me, all of them, right now.

"Please—" I gasped, "—I want..."

"What do you want, Karlee?" Taylor asked.

I glanced over Carson's shoulder and saw him standing naked, his thick cock in one hand, watching the three of us with a smirk. But he'd changed—not only was he naked, his skin wasn't white anymore. His skin had taken on a purple sheen, sparkling with light, as if he was radiating magic all around him.

I blinked, before realizing that Carson, too, was changing. His previously red hair had darkened to black, and his skin also shifted to purple, sparkling with an iridescent shimmer.

"What's this?" I stroked a hand along Carson's biceps, and he growled his appreciation.

"Can't keep our glamor up while we fuck," he answered roughly. "We need to give all our attention to you, now, lass."

He took my breasts with both hands and squeezed, brutally pinching my nipples until I moaned with pleasure, resting my head back against Lucas's shoulder and closing my eyes.

Okay, so they're sexy purple *Scottish men. Does that make any difference?*

"What do you want, Karlee?" Taylor asked again, closer this time.

I looked to my left—he was right next to me, still stroking his cock. The sexy smile on his face made me feel brave. I reached across and closed my hand around his. "I want this," I said, my voice low and husky with need. "I want to taste your cock."

He grinned. "On your knees."

Carson and Lucas backed off, unbuttoning their shirts and throwing their clothes aside.

If anyone came up here now, there'd be no way of denying what we were doing. It wasn't like back in the alley. Anyone walking in on this scene would know exactly what was going on. With a shiver of excitement, I realized that this was exactly what I wanted—the thrill of being caught, or at least, the potential risk.

I dropped to my knees, and Taylor grabbed my ponytail, guiding me towards his cock—also a light purple color, and sparkling with the same starlight as the rest of him. He pushed between my lips, hissing his appreciation as I licked along the length of his shaft. "Yesss," he hissed between gritted teeth. "You like my cock, Karlee?"

"Mmm," I hummed low in my throat. You taste like heaven.

He took my head in both hands and pushed further, grunting like an animal as he fucked my face.

At the same time, Carson and Lucas tugged at my clothes, unbuttoning my shirt and slipping it off me with graceful ease. Every rustle of cotton against my skin sent a shudder of desire through my body. They pushed me forward, so I was on all fours, and pulled my ass up higher in the air.

Carson moved behind me, bunching the waistband of my pants in his hands and pulling my ass back against him. "Do you want us to fuck you here, Karlee? Where someone could come up and see you being taken by three men?"

Taylor released me long enough for me to cry out, "Yes!" before thrusting back into my mouth again.

He leaned down and murmured in my ear. "You want someone to find us, Karlee? You want someone to see you being fucked by all of us at once?"

I groaned, bobbing back and forward on his cock as Carson yanked my pants down, baring my ass to the cold night air. He smacked his palm across my ass, quickly sinking his fingers inside me as I squealed in surprise.

"You're so wet, Karlee," Carson said. He swirled his fingers around, stretching me and pressing against my G-spot.

Lucas joined Taylor, also holding his hard cock out for me. Without them needing to ask, I took his in my hand and stroked it, pumping in time with Taylor's thrusts.

Carson pulled his fingers away and groaned. "You taste like honey. Makes me want more..."

His beard tickled my thighs just before he licked the whole length of my sex—no teasing, no working up, just flat-out drinking from me with so much enthusiasm, he was like a man possessed. He dived between my legs, spreading my ass wider so he could lick and suck at my clit.

I pushed back against him, desperate for some release, vaguely aware that I was getting louder now, less restrained, less worried about people coming up to the roof to see what the fuss was about. If anything, Taylor was right—I almost wanted them to come.

Taylor released my hair, pulling back and letting Lucas switch places with him. I explored his cock with all the passion I'd shown Taylor, swirling my tongue around the head and gazing up into those brown eyes. His lips curled, and he placed his hands on each side of my head, soaking up the view.

"Do you want us to fuck you now, Karlee?"

Yes, oh, fuck yes.

I moaned around his cock, my words muffled by him as he thrust deeper.

Carson took my clit between his lips and sucked, sending even more stars across my vision. My hips bucked against his face, grinding my pussy against his nose so hard I thought I'd suffocate him. But by that point I was past caring, past all rational thought. I had three men on me at once, in the cool night air, in plain view of more than one or two top-floor apartments, and it was heaven.

With a loud smacking sound, Carson released me, baring my cunt to the air again and leaving me hanging on the cusp of an amazing orgasm. But before I could complain, he slammed into me, sinking in so deep I could feel myself stretch to accommodate him. He gave me no time to think, no time to get accustomed to the sensation of him inside me—he took up a merciless rhythm, pounding me from behind so hard that his thighs smacked against my ass. With each thrust, he forced me forward on to Taylor's cock. I had to let go of Lucas to put both hands on the floor and stop myself from falling face first.

"So fucking tight," Carson growled behind me, clutching at the mounds of soft flesh on my hips and squeezing until it almost hurt.

My orgasm came barreling towards me all at once—pent up since last night and desperate for release, a long, high-pitched moan started in my chest and stretched out as they fucked me hard and fast.

Carson pulled out, and Lucas took his place. He sank inside me—gentler than Carson, but just as amazing.

"You're so into this, Karlee," Lucas said—and I heard the smile in his voice. "You're dripping for us."

Just his words were enough to stoke my desire again, sending me soaring as he pulled out, then sank slowly back in to me, sighing with bliss at the end of his stroke.

A car horn honked on the street below, and laughter bubbled up to meet us from someone unseen on the sidewalks.

"Just imagine them coming up here—" Lucas sank balls-deep into me again, "—and seeing you spit-roasted on our cocks."

Taylor reached around and grabbed my tits, squeezing my nipples as Lucas placed his fingers directly over my clit and rubbed in small, tight circles. They matched each other's rhythm, filling me simultaneously before leaving me empty and wanting again. I shuddered as another wave of pleasure streaked through me.

My pulse got louder in my ears, drowning out any sounds from the street below, even deafening me to Taylor's sexy murmurs of encouragement. I pushed back against them, circling my hips and taking the pleasure I needed. I squealed with delight as a second orgasm ripped through me, making me shudder all over, my pussy tightening around Lucas's cock.

"Fuck!" he thrust into me again.

"Do you want me to come in your mouth or on your tits, Karlee?" Taylor asked through gritted teeth.

I sucked harder, opening my eyes again and staring right up into his face. *Neither. I want you to fuck me.*

Taylor's eyes widened, and he pulled away. "Say that out loud." His low voice was so sexy, I would have done anything he'd asked me to. Even this.

"Fuck me," I said, waving my ass in the air, as if I needed to tempt him. The cold air licked against my wet cunt, chilling me to the bone but serving as yet another reminder of our exposed position. "I said I wanted you all to fuck me, and I meant it."

Taylor grinned. "Hell, yeah."

But instead of moving, he sat on his clothes and beckoned for me to join him. I straddled his lap, hovering just above his erect cock.

"How about you fuck me instead?" He breathed into my ear, nuzzling my neck.

"Oh, god..." I lowered on to him, my soaking wet cunt opening to accept him greedily. With aching slowness, I took him inside me and settled over him, panting with need and exhaustion—but I still wanted more.

"Take me," Taylor said, holding my hips to support me.

Carson and Lucas stepped to either side of us, stroking their cocks and raking their eyes over us.

Instantly I reached for them, pumping them in each hand as I bounced on Taylor's lap, relishing the feeling of him slamming deep inside me with each movement. The intense pressure on my clit had me climbing to orgasm within moments, quickening my pace and becoming more frenzied, less controlled.

The whole of New York faded to black as I came around him, my heart pounding in my ears, banging against the inside of my rib cage, only dimly aware of Lucas and Carson's hot cum landing on my chest and neck, their lips on mine, their hands pinching my nipples and slapping my ass.

Heaven.

KARLEE REBORN

I swirled my cocktail slowly in the martini glass, eyeing up the guy next to me with blatant appreciation. He was cute—tight jeans, tighter ass, latino maybe, well groomed but a little on the rugged side. Sort of reminded me of Lucas.

The sexy stranger side-eyed me, smirking slightly, before calling the bartender over.

"A beer for me, and whatever the lady's drinking." He leaned on the bar, turning to me with a rakish grin. "Having a nice night?"

"It got better when you came by," I said with a wink. "You alone?"

"I was," he reached for my shoulder, brushing a stray hair back behind my ear. A thrill of desire blossomed from where he touched me. "So, what are you into?"

I grinned at the direct question and raised an eyebrow. "You really wanna know?"

BEWITCHED BY DRYADS

ZARA JORDAN

FALLING

F alling from the cliff side wasn't so bad—the mountainous horizon lit up by the early sunrise, the wind whipping past my face, the squawk of the birds in the trees below me, the surreal feeling of weightlessness...

Of course, I wasn't much looking forward to the landing.

I flew in a strange mixture of slow motion and racing time—my heart pounding in my skull, a scream bubbling up from deep within me, echoing around the vast Welsh valleys with no one to hear. And yet, no matter how fast I was traveling, I had the time to endure every single one of my regrets—not spending enough time with my friends, losing the confidence to go out and find love again, or hell, even just good sex!

And probably my biggest regret, wearing crocs to climb the mountain.

The canopy below hurtled towards me, my long blond hair whipping in my face. I uttered my last prayer to whatever god, omnipotent llama, or spaghetti monster cared to listen. Then I squeezed my eyes shut and waited for the inevitable.

My landing was much less painful than I'd expected—and almost *soft*, as if the momentum had been diminished by the ground, like a shock absorber.

I must be dead, then.

Expecting the worst, I opened my eyes and found that I wasn't on the ground at all. I was still in the air, and I wasn't alone.

A massive creature covered in shimmering silver scales had caught me on its back. In a sudden panic, I gripped the fringe of iridescent plates that ran along its spine, using them like a harness. The large muscles underneath the scaly skin twitched in response.

"Ouch!" A booming voice struck me like thunder. Beyond the mass of its scaly body, a head turned back to regard me with one large cool gray eye. Its snout was long and pointed, and when it opened its mouth to speak, the teeth were sharkish—as in, this thing had too many of them. "Go easy on me, sweetheart. I'm only trying to help."

A tiny gasp got stuck in my throat, and I let go, holding my hands up in the air.

I guess I'd like to amend my biggest regret from earlier.

Unable to hold on, I slipped from the back of the gigantic beast, scrambling for a handhold on its smooth scaly hide. But there was nothing else to grab—the plates were sliding rapidly out of sight as I tumbled over its thighs, down to the end of its clawed feet.

The horizon flip-flopped in my hazy vision, making me lose my bearings... and possibly my breakfast.

"Whoah!" the monster boomed again, and its massive clawed foot reached for me, encircling my whole body in a warm, firm embrace. "Watch it! Let's get you back on solid ground."

With my arms pinned to my sides, and my entire body held in its vice-like grip, there was nothing I could do to disagree. Instead of speaking, I settled for gaping, fishlike, at the mythical beast that was carrying me to... safety?

From my position in its hind foot, I stared at the bottom of its long, bulky form—like a lion, but covered in a scaly hide, shimmering silver that reflected the peachy sunrise. It had four muscular legs, each ending in a lizard-like clawed foot with four toes.

A dragon.

Not the kind of dragon I was used to—mythical creatures that lived under mountains, terrorizing the local towns until a hero came to destroy them.

This was a real, live dragon.

Either that, or I was dead, and literally getting hauled off to some kooky afterlife with monsters and shit.

After taking me on a terrifying flight over the mountains, it flapped its monstrous wings and lowered me to the ground. It only released me when my feet were firmly planted on solid earth, but the second it let go, my knees gave in, and I collapsed in a wobbly mess.

I kneeled at the steps of a tiny cafe, perched on the top of the mountain peak next to a public footpath. The building itself was no bigger than a small shack, made of wood and large glass panes that allowed visitors to gaze out on the countryside. It looked empty. Outside, a patio surrounded the cafe, covered in more tables and chairs—also empty.

"Fancy a cuppa?" A man asked behind me.

I whirled around and found myself face-to-thigh with a tall, broad-shouldered guy with long gray hair tied in a topknot.

His gray eyes sparkled with humor as he looked me up and down. "Or maybe you need a little longer to catch your breath?"

"Who are you?" I panted.

"Arwel." He held out a hand and helped me to my feet. "And you are?"

"Gwen..." I glanced around, searching the horizon for any sign of the giant creature that had rescued me. But the mountains were silent, save for the birds and sheep "Did you see a—"

"Dragon?" He grinned. "That would be me. You're welcome, by the way."

The doors to the cafe burst open, and a man wearing a barista's apron came rushing down the steps, muttering to himself.

Great, at least someone else saw this. Now I can make sure I'm not going crazy.

I pointed to Arwel and gave the barista a questioning look. "Did you see?"

"He's lucky half of Brecon didn't see!" he shouted, waving his hand in the air to motion to the silent mountains. His copper curls shook on his head, glinting in the sun. "What the fuck you playin' at, Arwel?"

"Sorry Dylan." Arwel, who I realized still had my hand in his, grinned in a way that suggested he wasn't sorry at all. "Just needed to stretch my wings for a bit."

Dylan rolled his eyes. "And when the reports come in about a dragon 'stretching their wings' all over the Brecon beacons, I'm gonna be the one who has to explain it all to the MP."

Arwel gave him a sheepish look. "Sorry, Dylan."

"Ugh." Dylan closed his eyes and took a deep breath to calm himself. Then he turned to me. "And who's this?"

"Ah, my bad. Dylan, this is Gwen. Gwen—"

"What the fuck is going on?" I squealed, looking between the two men. "I was walking up the mountain and the next thing I know—"

"You fell," Arwel said. "You slipped from the edge and fell. Jesus, you're lucky you didn't *land*. You'd have been dead for sure."

"But you... You caught me? And you're a *dragon*?"

Arwel beamed at me. "Like I said, you're welcome."

At this, Dylan scoffed and beckoned for me to come into the cafe. "Come on, let's get you in the warm."

POKING THE DRAGON

I cradled a hot mug of coffee, with the most perfect latte art I'd ever seen in the foam—a perfect little dragon's tail swirling around the mug's edge. Dylan and Arwel sat at the table, observing me. They'd done a lot of talking, and I'd done my best to listen, but God... this was going to take some getting used to.

"So... dragons are real?" I muttered.

They nodded.

"And you're both dragons?"

They nodded.

"But nobody *knows*."

They nodded.

"And if I told someone—"

"They'd think you were crazy and not believe you," Arwel said. "But enough of us. What about *you*? What were you doing up here so early in the morning?"

This is just too fucking weird. Just go with it, Gwen.

"Well, I've been trying to get out more. I was just out hiking," I said, taking a sip of perfectly brewed coffee—hot, steaming bliss in a cup.

"In crocs." Arwel gave me a dead-ass grin.

My face burned. "Yeah, well... I don't hike much. I mean, that much is obvious." I motioned to my plus-sized body with a snort.

Usually, people joined in with my self-deprecation. Either they'd wave a hand and tell me off in a good-natured way, or they'd laugh along and move on.

They didn't usually glare at me like I'd killed a puppy right in front of them.

For a few long, silent moments, Dylan and Arwel stared at me with such intensity, it made me squirm in my chair.

"Don't do that," Dylan said, his golden eyes scorching a path down my neck, over my ample chest, then back up to meet my perplexed gaze.

I frowned. "Don't do what?"

"Don't criticize your body," Arwel answered, matching Dylan's burning scowl. "Don't put yourself down."

My mouth went dry—two total strangers telling me off for making a joke? And that turned me on... why, exactly?

"Sorry," I mumbled, staring into my cup like I could crawl into it and hide. "Old habit."

A shadow seemed to pass, and they relaxed, shaking off whatever anger had come over them.

Arwel reached for my shoulder, where his stupid, gigantic, clumsy dragon claw had ripped through the seams of my t-shirt.

"Sorry about your top." Heat throbbed where his fingers touched my shoulder.

A small, strangled cry rose in my throat at his touch, but I shook my head. "It's okay. It could have been worse... So... Are you—" I pointed to each of them and raised my eyebrows, hoping they can hear my thoughts so I wouldn't have to say it out loud and risk embarrassing myself.

Dylan frowned. "Are we what, love?"

I cleared my throat. "Like... together? Do you live up here, alone?"

"Two separate questions, Gwen." Arwel smirked, no doubt enjoying how awkward he was making me. "No, we're not *together*, and yes, we live here. It's easier to stay out of the way. Then if we fancy a flight—"

"—which we are only meant to do on a *strict* timetable." Dylan raised his eyebrows pointedly.

Arwel held up his hands. "Alright, alright, I fucked up. But if I hadn't, I wouldn't have seen Gwen. And she'd be lying broken on the side of a mountain right now."

Dylan's expression shifted from judgemental to guilty, and they gave me furtive glances.

"Sorry, Gwen," Meurig said. "I'm really happy Arwel saw you, but—"

"Not so happy I saw Arwel?" I smile, sipping the *heavenly* coffee again. "It's cool, I get it. This is all... a lot to take on board, if I'm honest. But that doesn't mean I'm not grateful."

I wanted so badly to figure out something I could do to thank Arwel—to thank both of them. Even though Dylan hadn't *literally caught me in mid-air*, they'd taken me in, wrapped me in a fleecy blanket and given me coffee and biscuits without question. Now my shakes had finally started to subside, my thoughts were clearing enough to start making sense of what had happened.

"So, can you both fly? And do you both change into..." I held my arms out and flapped them in a poor imitation of Arwel's massive wingspan.

Dylan nodded. "Yes, we both fly."

I frowned into my mug of coffee, trying to fit the pieces together. "I can't understand how you guys have gone unnoticed for so long. No one has seen you? Ever?"

At this, Dylan turned to Arwel again.

His tawny brown skin flushed as he stammered his excuses. "Yeah, well, you know, sometimes it's tricky to shift back in time and—"

"In front of a school bus full of children, Arwel?"

I couldn't help but smile at the casual way they continued bickering, like they'd known each other all their lives.

Arwel side-eyed me. "Can we not do this right now, *Dylan*?"

"Oh, don't mind me," I raised my hands and nudged my seat backwards, reaching into my pocket for my mobile as I made to stand up, clutching the ripped fabric of my shirt to preserve my dignity. "I'll be out of your hair right away. I'll just call a taxi—"

"What do you think you're doing?" Arwel's voice turned icy as he gazed at me.

"I'm... going?"

"You're not going anywhere," Dylan said, his tone as cold as Arwel's.

Oh, fuck. Oh, fuck oh fuck oh fuck. This is it. This is the part where they kill me. I know too much.

My chest heaved, hands trembling as I grabbed inside my pocket, desperately trying to find my phone and hold my clothes on at the same time.

My phone...

A crisp, high-definition image played in my mind of my mobile slipping from my pocket just as a massive dragon grabbed me from mid-air. It tumbled in slow motion towards the canopy of trees far, far below...

Oh fuck oh fuck oh fuck...

"People will be looking for me," I said, desperate to protect myself. "They know I'm up here and—"

Arwel stood, and it felt as if his tall, wide frame blocked out the sun for a moment. He walked in front of me and took my hand, pulling it towards him. Before I could protest, he placed his mobile phone into my palm. "Call them. Tell them you're safe, and to bring you some clothes."

I blinked at the phone a few times. "But you said I couldn't go..."

"You're not leaving here in *that*." He motioned to my top, which was now practically hanging down to my waist.

My confusion quickly replaced with burning anger, I scowled at him. "It was your stupid big claws that ripped it to begin with! Look, I know I'm no supermodel but—"

Everything happened at once.

Dylan grunted, sending his chair flying backwards as he stood abruptly.

Arwel placed his hand over my mouth, clamping it shut and preventing me from saying another word.

They closed in on me, their bodies so close to mine I could feel their heat on my skin, their breath on my face. Arwel's hand had changed—whereas it had been a normal, human hand, with strong fingers and well trimmed nails, it was now covered in shimmering scales. Silver and white, with a reflective rainbow of color. Just like when he caught me, it wasn't *cold*, but a warm, soft embrace. At the tips of his fingers, his nails extended to sharp white claws, which pressed into my cheek. At any moment, he might sink them into my flesh and cut me open.

To make it worse, all this attention from these two strangers was exciting me in a way I'd never experienced before. At least, not with another person.

I became aware of nothing more than my pounding heartbeat, my increasing need for oxygen, and the scorching heat of Dylan's golden eyes glaring at me.

Arwel leaned in close and held my gaze—his dark gray eyes daring me to protest. "Not. Another. Word."

FLIGHT PLANS?

T he dry mud crumbled under my crocs, making me skid
downhill as I raced down the mountain footpath, desperate to
get as far away from the two crazies behind me as I could.

"Gwen!" They chased me. But without the benefit of a head start,
they lagged behind.

I whipped tree branches backwards and dodged around trunks as
often as I could, hoping to hide myself in the forested embankment.

But there was no way I'd lose them. I was already out of breath,
sweat dripping down my spine, panting so heavily, I felt like I could
pass out at any moment.

What the hell were they playing at? What *was* that?

In ordinary circumstances, I would have run away from them the
second they first snapped at me. You don't talk to strangers like that. It
was just... *weird*. And all because, what, I was making jokes?

Fucking weirdos. No wonder they lived out here, alone.

And yet, they'd had me in their clutches, held enraptured with a
single command. *Why* hadn't I just left?

When they were circling me, it felt like being in the coils of a snake,
like I was their prey, held still while they decided what to do with me.
And I *wanted* them to do something with me, oh so badly.

I skidded to a stop near a bend in the path and leaned back against the rock face for a moment, desperate to catch my breath.

As my heavy pants slowed out and the buzzing in my head subsided, another sound caught my attention. A loud whoosh of air, like standing in front of a massive speaker pounding out a bass beat. But slower, much slower. Like the beating of gigantic wings...

I looked up, gritting my teeth at my stupidity.

Hovering twenty feet above my head, a massive golden dragon beat its wings, *somehow* remaining in the air, even though it seemed a million times less probable than even the fattest of bumblebees. Its massive, deep golden eyes stared me down as it lowered to the ground.

"Are you done?" Dylan's voice boomed, blowing my hair back from my face. "Or should I let you run off another cliff?"

"I did not *run* off a cliff."

"Mhmm," the dragon grumbled with a heavy note of sarcasm.

I could run, I could. But what was the point?

As I grabbed at the stitch in my side, wincing, the golden dragon shimmered in front of my eyes, like a mirage in the desert. Its image wavered and dissipated, leaving Dylan in its place.

"Why the hell are you chasing me?" I shouted. "You've only just met me!"

Dylan approached, looking intensely irritated—his jaw was set, clicking repeatedly as he tried to find the right words. Or maybe he was reconsidering his choices. "If you saw someone about to jump off a bridge, and you stopped them, would you let them go right away?"

I frowned. "Well... no... But I wouldn't stalk them like I was about to slaughter them, either?"

"Slaughter?" Dylan blinked, the anger fading suddenly. "We weren't going to *hurt* you."

"Oh no? What was all the... Touching, and... and *circling* about, then?"

Dylan pressed in close, brushing a stray hair back from my forehead with a concerned frown. I flushed with shame, intensely aware of how disheveled I must look right now, my lumpy figure revealed through my shredded top, long hair tangled and probably stuck with leaves, a sheen of sweat covering me from head to toe from my short sprint.

"I'm sorry," Dylan said, his face so close to mine that he could lean in and kiss me any moment...

I swallowed. "What?"

"Sorry about the... 'circling'. It's a... *thing* we do. It's hard for us to hold back from our instincts when we find someone we want."

"Someone you... What?"

Dylan smiled. "Come with me? Back to the cafe. I swear we won't hurt you. But out here, you're going to get lost, or maybe fall again."

I bit my lip, battling between my common sense and my libido.

On the one hand, they could be crazy.

On the other, they were both very sexy. And what was that about wanting me?

They might want to kill me, or eat me, or rip me to shreds to sacrifice me to some dragon god... Thing.

But they'd saved my life, kept me warm, and offered me a phone to call home.

I put my hand into Dylan's, expecting him to walk me back up the hill.

Instead, he grinned, and a flash of golden scales filled my vision, coiling around my body and squeezing me tight. A single shining claw as big as my arm curled around my legs, the pointed tip resting just at the apex of my thighs. I gulped, freezing solid with fear as the golden dragon formerly known as Dylan grabbed me and took off, allowing me a full view of the valley shrinking below me.

I might have screamed.

I may have whooped and grinned as crazy tears rolled down my cheeks.

There may have been a moment where I held my arms, which Dylan didn't have enclosed in his massive claws, up above my head like I was riding a rollercoaster, and "Wooooo"'d all the way back to the cafe.

By the time Dylan placed me on the ground again, I was a panting mess of adrenaline.

I watched him shift, transfixed by the way his body undulated and shimmered, changing from the enormous beast into a human—normal, apart from those beautiful, golden eyes.

Dylan snaked an arm around my waist and pecked me on the cheek. "Have fun this time?"

I grinned. "Maybe just a little."

A FAVOR

"Yes, I'm fine, mam, I promise."

"I *told* you to get some proper boots first, didn't I?" Even through my mother's I-told-you-so voice, I could hear her obvious relief. "Where is the cafe again?"

"Right at the peak, about a mile up the track from the national park center."

"We'll fetch a few bits up for you soon, love."

"Thanks mum."

I handed Arwel's phone back to him with a sheepish smile. "Thanks."

He nodded, tucking the blanket in around my shoulders while Dylan fussed around making coffee and breakfast. Their attention was gentle and loving—nothing like the carnal sexuality they'd exuded before I ran. They switched course so often; it was impossible to tell what version of them I was going to see next.

I couldn't decide if I hated that, or loved it.

"How long will it take her to get here?"

"She lives about two hours away, so it'll be a while." I winced. "You're *sure* it's okay for me to stay here all morning?"

"Gwen." Arwel motioned to the empty cafe. "There's no one else here. It's fine. You're doing *us* a favor."

"Oh, really?" I raised one eyebrow. "And what would that be?"

"Well, there's the chance to get to know you, for one." Arwel counted on his fingers. "The excuse to adore your sexy curves, for another..."

I blushed, but pressed my lips together, resisting the urge to butt in with a joke.

"Oh! And, let's not forget," Arwel leaned in close and pointed at Dylan. "The chance to take the piss out of Dylan for breaking his own flight rules!"

Dylan growled. "You should have run faster."

"You were running, too."

"I don't have trainers on."

"Neither do I."

I chuckled as they continued their friendly banter, settling into the warm sofa and cradling another warm cup of heaven.

I realized how much I enjoyed just *watching* them. They moved with such a strange grace, like lions stalking their prey—even when they were just fetching a cup from the shelf or something equally mundane. Their looks contrasted each other completely; Happy-go-lucky Arwel with his tall, dark and handsome routine—wide shoulders, long wavy black hair, and smoldering gray eyes. Surly Dylan, with his curly blonde locks and short stature, startling golden eyes and surly attitude.

They looked so at odds with their personalities. At a first glance, I easily would have assumed Dylan would be the cheerful one, but he was by far the grumpiest of the pair.

Although I swore I'd heard him chuckle when he had me in his claws, flying over the mountain tops...

"A penny for your thoughts," Arwel said, plopping onto the sofa next to me.

"Ah, I was just thinking about how it's been a weird day."

"Weird?" Arwel grinned. "How so?"

"Well, the dragon thing aside, Falling off a cliff and the whole, near death experience. And facing possible death-by-flight twice in a row with two sexy strangers."

Woah, Gwen... What the fuck is in this coffee?

Arwel grinned, but all the humor drained from his face—his smile was more predatory than anything I'd seen from him so far. "Sexy, huh?"

I gulped. "Maybe... just a little."

The sofa cushion dipped on my other side as Dylan joined us, his devious smile matching Arwel's. "You liked the flight then, Gwen?"

He took my cup from me, sliding it on to the coffee table in front of us.

"I, uh..." My pulse quickened, words failing me as they closed in on either side, their proximity dizzying me. "I guess."

"Is there anything else you'd like from us?" Dylan asked.

"What do you mean?"

Arwel tilted his head, craning his neck so his lip brushed my ear. "Well, for one thing, we've wanted to fuck you since the second you stepped through that door, Gwen."

I gasped as a rush of desire flushed my skin, prickling at the back of my neck. I wished they would just touch me already, but they continued the torture, keeping their hands away, leaning in close enough to kiss, but hovering just out of reach.

Dylan inhaled deeply, giving almost a sub-sonic groan that spoke directly to my aching core. "If you want to, of course."

I groaned, heat pooling between my legs. "Will you just shut up and kiss me already?"

Spell broken.

GWEN, CORRUPTED

They grinned, closing in on me as one and covering me in biting kisses, drawing sharp gasps of excitement from me. Arwel nuzzled my neck, nipping and sucking just to the point of pain before moving further down to my collarbone.

Dylan took my chin between his thumb and forefinger and kissed me, deepening it further when I mewled into his mouth. His tongue changed as we kissed. It became longer, and smoother, pushing further into my throat until my eyes rolled with overwhelming ecstasy.

"You're new to this," Arwel murmured, shifting away slightly. "So we'll go slow. Open your eyes, Gwen."

Dylan released me, and I turned to look at Arwel, who leaned back on the sofa, stroking his stiffening cock with one hand. My jaw dropped at the sight—long, thick ridges swirled around the shaft, meeting at the back where the flesh puckered and swelled, forming a line of large bumps. The head was elongated and flared in a way that made my pussy clench at the thought of taking him inside me.

"Is this okay?" Arwel asked, his gaze warm and inviting. "We *look* human in this form but there are still some—" He smirked. "—differences."

I chuckled slightly, but nodded. "This is *absolutely* okay. It's just... I haven't really done anything that exciting in the sex department."

Wow. Way to put it all out there, Gwen.

But I couldn't help it—I was worried. Worried that I wouldn't be enough. That I'd be *too much.* That my inexperience would be too obvious. No, I wasn't a virgin, but the most exciting thing I'd done in the bedroom was lie the other way around on the bed. Now I had two men—two *dragons*—telling me they wanted to fuck me.

"Relax," Dylan stroked my shoulder, tugging the tattered folds of my shirt aside and sliding his hand down my arm. "Let us take the lead. We'd prefer that, anyway."

"Okay..." I hummed as Dylan moved my hand to his crotch. The growing bulge of his cock radiated heat to my fingers. Tentatively, I unzipped his trousers and reached inside.

Arwel took my other hand and guided me to him, until I had them both in my grasp, marveling at their intense body heat, the firm ridges and bumps under my fingers, the growing bulges at the base of their cocks, just above their balls.

Arwel and Dylan groaned at my touch, thrusting into my hand. As I stroked them, I noticed their skin shifting in the light—traces of scales appearing merged with their skin, covering their arms, their chests, until they both glistened with silver and gold, weakening at my touch, unraveling in front of me. It was like they were losing control, and whatever glamor had masked their form was wavering.

It made me bold.

Licking my lips, I bent double and took Arwel into my mouth, satisfied at the loud gasp of pleasure that he gave. He reached for my hair, wrapping it around one of his hands and tugging me onto the floor. I kneeled, bobbing my head up and down along his thick, ridged shaft, whimpering at the thought of it filling me, dragging along my walls and stretching me around it.

A sharp scratch on my arm—Dylan had shifted his hands into claws, cutting through my t-shirt and slicing the tatters of material off me. He ran his hands over my back, groaning softly. "So fucking sweet, Gwen. Your skin is so soft. I'm dying to taste your cunt."

I moaned, grasping the base of Arwel's cock in one hand and doubling my efforts—sucking him harder, relaxing my throat and pushing him to the back until I felt close to gagging.

Dylan moved behind me and grasped my hips, pulling my ass up in the air. With one swift movement, he pulled my trousers down to my knees. He gripped my thighs, his claws digging into the soft mounds of flesh at the tops of my legs. I moaned and shifted my knees apart for him.

The second I'd moved, his vice-like grip released, and he licked slowly along the full length of my slit. He growled low in his throat, a sound that reminded me of horror movies, and sucked on my clit, making me buck against him.

"See, Gwen, maybe you're not as sweet as we think you are," Arwel murmured, pulling the back of my head so his cock rammed into my throat.

I groaned loudly, wiggling against Dylan's tongue and grinding my clit on his chin.

"Maybe you are a kinky little thing, after all," Arwel said, thrusting deeper.

Oh, fuck yes. Something inside me woke up. Some long-lost flicker of excitement and adventure became a blazing flame, fueled by their heat, fed by their lust.

Dylan grabbed my hips again, his claws sinking in, and drove in deeper, fucking me with what I could only imagine was an inhumanly long, unnaturally *strong* dragon tongue. The contrast between his smooth, silky tongue stroking my inner walls, and Arwel's ridged, bulging dick in my mouth drove me into autopilot, bouncing between them both with insatiable need, climbing higher and closer to an orgasm I felt like I'd been chasing for years.

"Such a good girl," Arwel groaned, holding me my the roots of my hair and gyrating against my chin.

A flush of pride tickled my neck, spreading down my chest and driving me to work harder, bobbing up and down on his cock like my life depended on it.

There was no way I'd ever be able to take all of him in my mouth—the base of his cock swelled even more as our movements became more frantic, stopping me from taking more than half of his shaft into my mouth.

"Do you think you could take all of this in that gorgeous, tight cunt, Gwen?" Arwel murmured, pulling away and leaving my mouth free.

I shivered at the possibilities; the challenge posed by his intimidating girth, but nodded breathlessly. "I'll try."

Dylan stood up, grabbing my hands and spinning me around to face him. He ran a single sharp claw down my cheek with a smile, gazing at my mouth. "Your lips are so swollen, Gwen."

He leaned in and took my lower lip between his teeth, biting gently enough to make me move towards him without using a finger.

Between them both, they bent me double, so I'd switched sides—Arwel stood behind me, grasping my hips, while Dylan pressed down gently on my shoulder, guiding my face to his dick, hard and ready, with even deeper ridges and bulges along its length. I wrapped my lips around him eagerly, just as Arwel pressed against my opening, pausing briefly.

"Are you ready for me, Gwen?"

I moaned in reply, tilting my hips back towards him in an invitation. He chuckled, circling my hips with both hands and thrusting forward, filling me so quickly I barely had a chance to feel the hard ridges, the bumps—the only thing I felt was *full*, blissfully so. My hips bucked in response, and he stilled inside me as I adjusted to the new sensations.

Dylan flexed his hips, dragging his thick cock over my tongue while I temporarily blacked out from all reality. "Is everything okay, love?"

A low, drawn-out hum was all I could manage in response, as I wiggled my hips, aware that even now, Arwel still hadn't fully penetrated me—the swollen base of his cock stretched my opening, and with each movement, the ridges dragged along my G-spot.

They set the pace together, taking control of my body like I was their puppet, sliding in and out of my mouth, my cunt, gripping my hips and holding my hair.

I got so lost in their rhythm that I barely realized Arwel had pressed further, pushing the swollen base of his cock inside me, stretching me a little more each time. The momentary burn gave way to an intense jolt of pleasure, and I met his thrusts, pushing back against him, allowing him deeper inside me with each movement.

"Ah!" Arwel pulled back suddenly, leaving me gasping for more as he clutched my hips, dragging his cock between my ass cheeks with a sigh. A moment later, a hot pool of cum gathered in the small of my back.

A tiny whine escaped me. Dylan chuckled, pulled me back by my hair. "Still hungry for more, sweetheart?"

He teased my lips with the head of his cock, keeping me firmly in his hold while I panted, trying to find the words. He raised his eyebrows at me, and I knew he wouldn't give me what I wanted until I asked for it.

"Yes," I gasped. "Please, fuck me."

Arwel slapped me on the ass and moved for Dylan to take his place. I barely had a moment to breathe before he plunged inside me, sinking in with a low rumble of satisfaction.

"Your cunt feels as good as it tastes, Gwen," Dylan groaned.

I writhed against him, desperate to feel him deeper inside me, feel him stretch me so wide I might tear apart.

Dylan leaned over me, forcing me down to all fours, my chest almost touching the floor. "I'm going to fuck you hard," he growled. "So hard you'll be covered in bruises by the evening. Is that what you want?"

"Oh, fuck yes." The voice coming out of my mouth didn't even sound like my own anymore. It's like I was possessed—whatever this hypnotizing power they had over me was, I wanted more of it, all of it. I wanted them to claim me and fill me until I couldn't see straight anymore.

Dylan chuckled, placing his palm between my shoulder-blades and pushing me even lower. My face pressed into the floor, my ass still in the air. He took my wrists in his hand and dragged my arms behind my back, sinking ever so slightly deeper inside me at the same time.

I moaned at the delicious stretch of his cock inside me, wriggling back against him, desperate for more. Dylan squeezed my wrists together with one hand and spanked my ass with the other. "Just let go, Gwen. I want to feel you coming apart around my cock."

And with that, he pulled back, and slammed into me, pulling back on my arms. As he drew slowly back again, his rippled cock dragged along my inner walls, making me shudder and moan for more. And he slammed into me again, sinking in further, stretching me and grinding at the end of the stroke, so the swollen bulge at the base of his cock *almost* sank inside me.

Again and again, he pulled out slowly before ramming me into the ground. Next to us, Arwel lounged on the sofa, watching with a massive grin on his face as he stroked himself, already getting hard again at the sight of Dylan pounding into me from behind.

"You look so beautiful like this, Gwen," Arwel said. "Keep watching me. I want to watch your eyes cross when Dylan sinks all the way in to you."

I struggled to keep him in focus as Dylan quickened his punishing rhythm, grinding his hips into my ass. A low hum built in my chest as my orgasm climbed again, building more with each thrust.

"That's it, baby, let go for me." Dylan kept up his merciless pace, not slowing for a second even when I began to buck and writhe against him.

I clenched around him, gasping as the ridges of his shaft massaged every pleasure center within me, drawing out the agony, making me shudder and moan.

"Come for me, Gwen. Grip my cock tight with that beautiful, delicious pussy of yours." Dylan said through clenched teeth, circling his hips.

"Ah! Fuck, yes!" I clenched tighter around him, grinding my hips back so the swollen base of his shaft rubbed against my clit. Stars danced in front of my eyes as I came, shouting a stream of obscenities as Arwel grinned down at me, stroking his amazing cock with scaly, clawed fingers.

Dylan let my arms go, grabbing my hips and ramming into me, riding me through my orgasm, pushing me higher with each thrust, extending the pleasure and stimulating me more until I was sure I would pass out.

Just as my vision began to blacken, he pulled out and grunted, soaking my back with his cum.

I sank down to the floor, my knees slipping under me, a smile spreading across my face.

"Oh, Gwen," Arwel groaned. "You look so damn sweet with that just-fucked look on your face."

I wanted to reach for him, but my body had given in, completely spent and breathless.

Dylan planted a soft, sweet kiss on my shoulder. "We could do this again, sometime. If you like."

I grinned, feeling drunk in my hazy afterglow. "Fuck, yes."

EXCITEMENT; 3,560FT

I cradled my mobile between my ear and my shoulder, cleaning the coffee machine until it gleamed. "Hey, Dianne, it's been a while!"

It had actually been more than 'a while'. It had been years since I last spoke with my college friend, but she was good enough to forgive me for it.

"So I saw you posted a bucket list," Dianne drawled. "How is your little 'adventure seeking trip' going?"

Dylan walked by me, leaning over to give me a peck on the cheek before going back to serve a group of hikers. I grinned at his ass as he walked away. "Good actually," I said. "I'm trying new things every day."

Arwel moved behind me, squeezing my ass and coming close enough for me to feel the telltale bulge in his pants. He reached past me to the coffee hopper and took off the lid, before kissing me on the neck, careful to avoid drawing attention.

"And you're really okay working in a cafe in the middle of nowhere?" Dianne continued, blissfully unaware of the mauling Arwel was subjecting me to on the other end of the phone. "How do you find *any* excitement up there, really?"

I grinned at the sound of Arwel's zipper. "You'd be surprised."

ABOUT ZARA JORDAN

Fluffy or slimy, tentacled or tusked, If anything gets Zara hot under the collar, it's helping her horny fantasy characters to live out their best lives.

When she isn't writing dark, delicious smut, Zara enjoys conducting seances for her many past lovers, gathered at the full moo— okay yes she drinks ridiculous amounts of coffee and drools over horror flicks, happy now?

More by Zara Jordan

Like what you see?

Find more of my sexy monster shorts, all available for purchase and to read on Kindle Unlimited, on my <u>amazon author page</u>

More in the Monster Mash Series:

(Paranormal Ménages & Reverse Harems)

<u>Shared by Orcs</u>

Printed in Great Britain
by Amazon